NEW VOICES

FROM

aunt lute

1

featuring
DeeAnne Davis
Rabie Harris
Gloria Yamato

guest editor
Sauda Burch

aunt lute books
SAN FRANCISCO

First Edition
10 9 8 7 6 5 4 3 2 1

Aunt Lute Books
P.O. Box 410687
San Francisco, CA 94141

This book was funded in part by a grant from the National Endowment for the Arts. This is a work of fiction. In no way does it intend to represent any real person, living or dead, or any real incidents.

Cover, Text Design and Typesetting: Pamela Wilson Design Studio

Guest Editor: Sauda Burch
Senior Editor: Joan Pinkvoss
Managing Editor: Christine Lymbertos

Production:	Cristina Azócar	JeeYeun Lee
	Vita Iskandar	Kathleen Wilkinson
	Heather Lee	

Production Support:	Denise Conca	Melissa Levin
	Irma de Jesus	Norma Torres
	Jonna K. Eagle	Michelle Uribe
	Jamie Lee Evans	Alexa Weinstein

Printed in the U.S.A. on acid-free paper.

Library of Congress Cataloging-in-Publication Data
Davis, DeeAnne, 1962-
    New voices from Aunt Lute 1 / featuring DeeAnne Davis, Rabie Harris, Gloria Yamato : guest editor, Sauda Burch.
        p. cm.
    ISBN 1-879960-38-9 (pbk. : alk. paper). — ISBN 1-879960-39-7 (lib. bdg. : alk. paper)
        1. American literature—Afro-American authors. 2. American literature—Women authors. 3. American literature—20th century. 4. Afro-American women—Literary collections. 5. Afro-Americans —Literary collections. I. Harris, Rabie, 1944- . II. Yamato, Gloria, 1953- . III. Burch, Sauda. IV. Title.
PS508.N3D4   1995
810.8'09287'08996—dc20   95-13818
                                                                CIP

Editor's Note

New Voices was conceived as a way to bring new writers into print who have not yet been able to produce a novel on their own but whose shorter pieces show considerable talent. Our plan is to showcase two to four authors in an annual collection of new talent. But the idea of *New Voices* goes beyond the book itself. Aunt Lute understands that writers need nurturing; they need audiences who will give them feedback and spur them on to write. Because *New Voices* is a work in progress, the writers welcome your feedback, either as they travel around the country reading, or in letters you send to them through Aunt Lute. Ongoing dialogue is always an important part of a writer's development.

This first book in the *New Voices* series features authors DeeAnne Davis from Oakland, Rabie Harris from Houston and Gloria Yamato from Seattle (who has just resettled in the Bay Area). Though all three identify as African American writers, we never intended to group authors by similar cultural experience. Rather, this particular grouping was the product of a selection process of Aunt Lute's new Manuscript Acquisitions and Development Committee, choosing the best talent from manuscripts available to them at the time. Future *New Voices* may see authors of different communities and races under the same cover.

We are delighted with the depth and range of talent from these three unpublished writers. Their subjects are as strikingly unusual and varied as the forms they've chosen. They have set the tone of excitement that readers will come to expect from the *New Voices* series.

April 1995

Acknowledgments

I'd like to send my heart to the Clothilde Sisters who have taught me that there is no shame in the truth. To my family and the community of those who love and support me, thank you for your continuing encouragement, laughter and the shared tears. We must all keep believing.

DeeAnne Davis

For opening the way, I thank the Ancestors whose solid support and inspiration I have felt throughout this process.

For opening the way, I also thank Aunt Lute Books, especially Joan Pinkvoss, Sauda Burch and Chris Lymbertos for their constant encouragement and generosity.

For being there for me all along the way, my deepest appreciation to my family and extended family, especially Tatsu, Ahmad and Masaaki Yamato, the Jacksons, Judy Ballantine, Doug Blane, Juliette Brown, William Covington III, L.A. (Babyface) Conner, Valerie Curtis Newton, Lisa Hall, Cheryl Harrison, C. Hill, Eleanor Palacios, Red and Black Books, C. Singing Arrow, the Specific Passions crew, Loren Smith, A Territory Resource, Lisette Womak.

Gloria Yamato

Thanks to Paul Ireland, my friend who helped me through the intricacies of putting *Diary of a Journey* into the computer, who edited and comforted me and would have been glad to see *Diary* published; Sauda Burch for her sincerity in preserving what she saw as strengths, for her advice and questions which helped me get to the heart of *Diary* by re-examining my intent for writing the piece; Rosellen Brown for her thoughtful suggestions and guidance in helping me complete this work; Philip Lopate for his support and encouragement while I was writing *Diary* more than ten years ago; Beatrice Patterson, the heart of *Diary.*

Rabie Harris

I am excited to be a part of the first *New Voices* anthology. I would like to thank the women at Aunt Lute Books for their support during the editing process. A special thanks to Joan Pinkvoss for approaching me about guest editing this first volume and for sharing with me her ample experience and knowledge throughout. I would also like to thank my life partner, Xochipala, for her constancy and unerring support of my writing and my dreams. My sincere gratitude to the three women whose writing is represented in this anthology: Rabie, Gloria and DeeAnne, for their willingness to work and stretch with me; I am grateful for all that I have learned. Aché.

Sauda Burch

TABLE OF CONTENTS

NEW
VOICES

DeeAnne
Davis

Burgundy Night Skies

CHAPTER ONE

The hot night air breathed a heavy sigh through the open windows of the cab. The streets lay low in shadow, caught under the glare of intermittent streetlights. Eugene looked out the window and saw the trappings of his own dislocation. The street was lined with cars with red tape for brake lights and silver tape for the sheets of plastic stretched over broken and missing windows. Broken-down cars, stripped of their tires and windows, trunks ajar, had taken up permanent parking places along the street, sometimes one behind the other. Nothing was ever hauled away from this part of the city, except what could be crushed into a trash can and carried to the curb once a week. The visible evidence of hopelessness was left to rust and grow weeds, considered too much trouble to cart away. But despair was also hidden here, mushroomed into heaps transparent and so deep that the roots were twisted and practically impossible to find.

Eugene reached for *Kind of Blue* from the case beside him and pushed the tape into the deck. He liked improvisational jazz for these long runs through his emotions. Following Coltrane on sax led him in a completely different direction than Evans on piano or Miles on trumpet. It was loneliness that picked at Eugene, chipped away at him. He had a date later, which usually kept his spirits up, but he was tired of dating—a fabulous man—but one who after a year still wanted to call their relationship "getting together."

He patted the sweat from his forehead and above his collar with the hand towel laying across his thigh. He refused to get the air conditioning fixed. He never liked the blasts of cold air. It had always bothered him, though he could never put his finger on why. It was like a dream lurking around his memory that he couldn't quite remember. Maybe it was because he didn't grow up with air conditioning, down in Georgia where it got mighty hot. Anyhow, when the unit in the cab up and stopped one day, something in him was put to rest, so he left it as it was.

Turning onto Halsted Street, Eugene pulled his cab, a sky blue Crown Victoria Ford LTD, to the curb to pick up his regular fare, Freddy Simmons.

"Hey now, Freddy. I can smell the cologne from here, man. Something *real* good must be meeting you at that parking lot tonight." Eugene laughed as Freddy leaned into the passenger window.

"Naw, man, I signed off. Heading down to Young & Foolish. They're holding an all night comedy competition. First place gets a job on the circuit. And you know that's me. That's got to be me, my man." Freddy opened the back door of the cab and slid his heavy frame into the back seat, pulling the car door closed. Eugene handed him a Coke from the cooler on the floor.

"Right on time, Gene," Freddy said, downing the soda in two large gulps. "Wish you'd fix the A/C, man."

"Told you I like the fresh air, Freddy."

"You call this fresh? I call it hot and muggy, like a rotting swamp, man, and that isn't close to fresh," Freddy badgered Eugene.

"You know I'm not going to get this thing fixed," Eugene countered, turning up the music.

"Okay, okay. Hey, isn't that Miles—playing 'Freddie Freeloader'? Used to be my calling card. Boy, that takes me back."

"Recorded in fifty-nine," Eugene informed Freddy. "I was nothing but a baby. How old were you?"

"You a lie, man," Freddy smirked.

They laughed, letting the subject of their ages dissolve into the music.

"Okay, Freddy, we're on it. Lead the way."

Freddy directed Eugene into an unfamiliar neighborhood. As they pulled up to the building, Eugene saw a half-lit marquee and a handful of weary people smoking cigarettes between sets.

"What do I owe you, man? Same?" Freddy held out a ten dollar bill and the empty Coke can.

"Same'll do, Freddy," said Eugene, taking the bill and the can.

"Hey, keep the change, Gene. My life's changing—tonight." Freddy slapped Eugene on the back and got out of the cab. Eugene tossed the can into a narrow recycling box next to the cooler and watched Freddy as he disappeared through the glass doors. This was not going to be Freddy's big break, just another half-baked scheme. I can wait to hear this sad story, he thought, shaking his head, and pulling away from the club. The city was full of sad stories.

Not like Fritz. Fritz was pure energy. Energy that fed Eugene's confidence, motivated him, inspired a playfulness in him. Eugene smiled, thinking back to their beginnings. He turned onto Lake Shore Drive and turned up the volume on the tape deck. Pulling thoughts of Fritz close to him, Eugene's head skipped, keeping time with Cobb on traps.

Fritz had gotten his break just over a year ago. He was a freelance photographer who was paying his rent by shooting weddings and location shots for brochures. Fritz worked to get a series of his photos, individual shots of black teenaged girls, displayed at a small gallery housed within a local community center. His exhibit happened to be the visual the media used for one of the mayor's press conferences. The topic of the press conference was buried under the hundreds of calls to the center and the mayor's office asking about the photographs, reviewed by one art critic as "a loud and plaintive cry from a generation forgotten." Now Fritz worked for the *Tribune* and freelanced when he could.

They had met at the center when Eugene went to see the exhibit. Standing behind a crowd of high school students and their teacher, Eugene watched Fritz talk about his work. Fritz read one photograph's inscription with a smile, as if the photo had captured a laughing girl instead of one whose forlorn expression was enough to bring tears to the eyes of some of the students.

"Shondra, mother of Johannes, two, is thirteen. She was born to fifteen-year-old Elizabeth who was born to twelve-year-old Mary. Shondra wants to be an actress..."

Six foot tall, Fritz wore silver-rimmed round glasses balanced on a ridge of high clay-colored cheekbones. He held his body tightly with a pronounced dancer's grace and spoke hurriedly as if he were rushed to make his next appointment. It was clear to Eugene that words could not speak for the experience Fritz had relating to these young girls. He would have done better to dance their stories, Eugene suspected, and he would have enjoyed watching. Eugene could see, even then, that Fritz was not a man of words. That's what attracted Eugene, the fluidity of Fritz's movements, the soft light framing his face as if he were enchanted, driven magically by his work.

Eugene stayed to introduce himself when the class moved on. He and Fritz made a date for coffee the next morning. A year later, they said they were still seeing other people, although Eugene's list had narrowed to one. He was meeting Fritz later to talk about it. He wanted this emptiness to move over, to make room for something more promising between them.

Eugene thought he had found his lifelong partner when he married Rex. Rex was college educated, a junior copywriter, strong-minded and beautiful. Any man's dream. His dream. He was a taxi driver with a high school diploma—a farm boy. It astonished Eugene that Rex could love him, still loved him after all they had been through. He left her because he felt he was a stranger to her, and to himself. He went looking for himself in a community of men where he hoped to find the spirit that would lift him beyond his own stagnation.

"Problem is," Eugene said aloud, "I just had the whirl-wind tour with the boys and I'm no better for it. I feel like I'm right back where I started."

Eugene adjusted the rearview mirror to see his face. I want to get married to a man. Sounds crazy. Are men supposed to want that?

As a young boy his grandfather, sitting in his work shed surrounded by the furniture he built and carved, told him how to work out his confusion. "Have a conversation with yourself first, boy," he'd say, "then come to me and tell me what you all decided." He'd add, making Eugene's hands into small fists, "Put one side of the argument in the left hand, the other in the right."

He taught Eugene the rhyme:

Eenie, meenie, minie, moe.
Catch a tiger by the toe.
If he hollers make him pay
fifty dollars every day.
My mama told me to pick
this very best one.

If the rhyme ended on the right side, he'd say, "Let it fly. Put it in the wind and the answer will land, by and by."

If Eugene picked the left side, his grandfather would say, "Best go with that, son. Left side made your decision today. Go on and act on it, and let me know how it turns out."

Eugene learned how to manipulate the rhyme so that if he wanted to do something about his confusion, he'd land on his left side, if not, the right.

Eugene spoke to himself in the mirror. "Is marriage the way out or is it just another trap?" Who did he know who had a family—and was happy—for god's sake?

He thought of Mona, the girl who lived across the street. She wasn't a child, but she sure needed a responsible adult in her life. He had seen her watching him, cataloguing his comings and goings. He figured she was looking for something to do and he was the neighborhood curiosity.

Her mother was quite a curiosity herself. A woman more drunk than sober, shouting for Mona whenever the girl was out of her sight. "MOOOna, git in here right now, girl, and help me like you s'posed to." The voice, a worn graveled road of alcohol and cigarettes, landed each time like a balled knot in his stomach. It took him back two years to the fists that had pounded unexpectedly into his middle.

Oddly, Mona was a support to him, a cornerstone adding a special touch to his edges. He'd catch himself thinking how nice it would be to help the girl believe in her own worth. Selfishly, though, he knew he hadn't been willing to break the spell of their invisible relationship. It was as if he were being loved by the daughter he never had and, vicariously, he accepted.

He remembered seeing Mona with only one other girl. She was strange, too, vacant eyes, and as quiet as Mona. Like two ghosts, those two. One moment an empty sidewalk, the next, they would appear leaning into their hips, doing nothing. He hadn't seen the other girl all summer.

Now it was just Mona, hanging out on the corner, lingering beneath his windows. She was small to begin with and wore baggy clothes that nearly swallowed her whole. She wore her hair in long copper-colored braids that hung in her face. Everything about Mona was camouflaged, and Eugene sometimes felt like he was the terrain she was stalking.

Maybe he should follow his impulses and befriend her. Fritz had become a mentor to many of the girls in his photographs. Eugene could let Mona know she had someone on the block, besides old Miss Cecile, who cared about her. Jesus, what did he know about helping a kid whose mother seemed to suck her in and spit her out every chance she got?

Eugene almost always chose to put indecision on the right side, the back burner. He recalled the years of growing up with his grandparents as an easy time. He followed simple routines: school, yardwork, feeding the chickens, selling eggs and watermelon by the roadside, bathing their collie, Sir. If anything ever went wrong, he always had a home to come back to.

There had been no place for him to go that night. After the beating. His folks were both dead. Grandad when Eugene was sixteen and Granny Pinky nine years ago. His mother was alive, but he had never gone there for anything. Eight kids besides himself. His grandparents raised him from the beginning; those were the only parents he knew.

Eugene yawned and ran his palm over his nubby hair, clipped down to his scalp. He glanced at his watch. He had about a half hour before his date with Fritz at midnight. Eugene turned off the main drive to check out an area above his neighborhood. For the last year, he had been working overtime to build his business. He got a beeper so his clients could page him, offered low fares, good music and free pop. He had established a steady base of customers and had slowed down a bit, but he always kept an eye out for new business.

The cab moved slowly through the nearly deserted and poorly lit streets. A group of young men clung together on one corner. Most of the houses were dark. It was Sunday night. Eugene knew that these were people who would be getting up and going to work in the morning. He decided to come through next weekend when he could catch folks at ease around their houses, a good time to talk and pass out his card.

Eugene nudged the mirror back into place and checked his rear. He turned the cab down a street bordering a high school football field, heading towards downtown, when his headlights caught the outline of what appeared to be two people fighting. One of the forms fell to the street. The standing figure continued to pummel the downed body with its fists.

Eugene felt panic rise from his gut into his mouth. Instinctively, he pressed down on the accelerator, looking straight ahead. Visions of his own beating, the men circling him, flooded his view. Halfway down the street he thought of Fritz, his grandparents. His foot rose off the pedal. Backing up, he slammed on his brakes, stopping the cab thirty feet from the scene. Eugene grabbed the tire iron he kept under his seat and got out of the car. He moved cautiously towards the figure standing guard over the crumpled body.

The man stood his ground for a moment, his short stocky legs spread like an immovable truck. Eugene could not see his eyes, but he could hear him breathing and feel the energy of his fury. The man retreated, skipping backwards, daring Eugene to come after him.

"The bitch deserved it, man. Someone needed to teach her a lesson," he yelled.

Eugene growled, running towards him, the tire iron held high over his head.

"You can have her," the man shouted, jumping the fence onto the field. "She's a little bitch, a tease. I shoulda took it from her, but she's not worth the ground I'd bloody." He turned and ran across the dark field into the night.

Eugene leaned on the fence to catch his breath. Then he rushed back to the body lying in the street. He saw a young girl, rolled into a fetal position, rocking herself against the curb.

CHAPTER TWO

Mona lay on the back seat of the cab in a tangle of long thick braids. Her fingers crawled up the right side of her jaw, a sloping hill leading to the swollen mass of cheekbone and half-closed eye. Her fingers flaked off the dried crust on her cheeks: tears, snot and blood sealed with a thin glaze of shining sweat.

The smell of fear is a warm animal in heat. The blood smell lingered in Mona's memory as she replayed the terror of the last few hours. Victor beating her, punishing her, chastising her as if she were a child. She remembered his fists smashing into her side, her face, and then he was gone and someone had picked her up from the curb. She hadn't opened her eyes to see who carried her away. She didn't care, as long as it wasn't Victor.

Now the man was beside her, shifting his weight. She gulped, the dry release between tears, as she thought of escaping this potential danger. But she didn't smell blood and she wasn't afraid. She couldn't move anyway. Every part of her body screamed for attention. She wanted to sleep, to forget Victor's betrayal, her own feeble attempts at defending herself.

Eugene had parked the cab on a dead end street, against a bridge of train tracks. He needed to think before he took Mona to the hospital. He pulled the front seat forward, making room for himself in the back with her. He sat on his knees, switching to his hip when his knees began to ache. He gently wiped Mona's face with a towel soaked in soda water.

Mona winced, the towel's wetness cool but painful against her raw face. A freight train passed overhead, rocking the earth, its shrill whistle piercing the air. Mona pushed Eugene's hand away roughly, her tight moans drowned out by the chugachuga of the disappearing train. She took up the sound and found a low vibration in her chest to ease her aching body.

She thought about the morning, which seemed distant and insignificant. She had stood in the shower, the water keeping rhythm against her back. Shutting her eyes tightly against the spray, she opened her mouth and shot sound to the ceiling. This was her morning ritual. Sometimes the words came sharp and spitting like darts rushing towards a bull's-eye. Other times words tripped clumsily, one on top of the other. When the sounds wove effortlessly into each other, falling like drizzling rain, an almost imperceptible "pooph" of song, she was trance-like, seduced into herself.

Beneath the warm spray, in the nasal column of the shower, Mona felt solid. This was her only haven from her mother's constant humiliation of her. Mona yearned for this now, an encircling womb, safe and warm and liquid.

What am I getting myself into? Eugene thought, peering into Mona's face. He was hesitant to take her to the hospital. People would stare at her, and they would want to know who he was. He still wasn't sure he wanted to become involved with this girl, but Mona had to go to the hospital. What choice did he have?

"Mona, it's me, Eugene, from across the street. I found you, honey. You're safe, you hear?" It was the first time he had ever spoken to her, addressed her by name. He liked the roundness of her name in his mouth. It wasn't harsh as he had heard it from her mother issued like a rocket out of her mouth.

Mona turned her head slightly towards the sound of Eugene's voice.

"I have to take you to the hospital. You're beat up pretty bad."

Mona stopped humming and breathing simultaneously.

"Soon...breathe, Mona. Come on with it." He applied gentle pressure to her stomach with the palm of his hand. She gasped, pulling at the air.

"You okay?"

Mona resumed a careful shallow breathing.

Eugene waited.

"Hey, I need you to talk to me. You've got to help me out here."

"I don't want to go. I can't go." Mona's fears spilled from her in panicked spurts. She wrapped herself in her arms.

"You've got to go, honey. But I won't leave you there. Lord knows I can't stand hospitals or doctors either. I'll stay with you, hold your hand—whatever you need." Eugene uncrossed Mona's arms and held her hands.

She pulled her hands away from him. "Victor said I deserved what I got. I ain't nothing to him." She wondered if she could trust this man she had been watching for so long. If I open my eyes, will I see someone who hates me, feels sorry for me or wants to help me?

Even with her doubts, Mona was desperate to see beyond the heavy blackness, to look up at the man who spoke her name so tenderly. She opened her eyes. He smiled at her. His teeth were as white and starched straight as the standup collar he wore buttoned to his throat. Up close, Eugene looked proper, too damn stiff. She could see that he felt sorry for her, his long eyelashes batting away some old guilt he wanted to get rid of. And that scar.

Mona narrowed her eyes into mean slits, erasing the smile from his lips. He's ugly up close, she decided.

"I don't want your help," Mona hissed at Eugene, closing her eyes.

Mona thought of Eugene by his name, but everyone in the neighborhood called him Cabbie. "You see Cabbie?" they'd ask. "Where's Cabbie when you need him? I got to be to church in ten minutes." "I sure wish Cabbie would hurry back to this stop."

The stop was an oil-stained twenty-foot length of curb in front of the two-story brownstone, reserved for the LTD that served as transportation for the residents of this corner of the city. Had been for the last two years, ever since that crazy beating by five or ten—no one knew exactly how many—white men out in Bridgeport. They said Eugene was taking a fare home, into the wrong neighborhood. When Eugene started driving again, he walked with a permanent limp and had a three-inch black scar on his left cheek where he had been sliced with a hunting knife. Since then Eugene's only business was his neighbors. They never saw his Yellow Cab again.

Watching Eugene, ever since his accident, was a pastime, a harmless escape. He lived on the second floor in the building across the street. She often smelled the hot spices of his cooking dripping out of the windows. More than once she had lurked in the corner of his apartment stairs between the brick building and the sidewalk, drinking the smell as if the food were liquid.

She knew Eugene liked men. She watched them approach: tall, elegant, dark-skinned men with wide chests and deepset eyes. She wondered where he had found so many who looked the same, like princes from the desert. But Eugene's men appeared for a short time and then disappeared forever. She had seen only one man more than once. He was the color of muted red clay, tall and slender like the others, and led with his chest when he walked. He never stayed over for long though, rushing into Eugene's building in the evening and running out early the next morning.

Then there was Rex. Mona knew her by name because Eugene would sometimes call after her when she was leaving. Mona liked that they kissed when Rex left. It meant he didn't hate women the way people said gays did. Miss Cecile told Mona that Rex was Eugene's ex-wife, she'd asked him straight out during one of her rides with him to church.

Eugene adjusted himself back onto his knees. His first impulse had been to push her back. She was in his cab, carried to safety in his arms, no less, and she was going to challenge him? A fifteen- or sixteen-year-old girl? Jesus!

He checked his watch, remembering that Fritz was waiting for him at the club. It was nearly one o'clock. "Dang, we have a hard time making this one work, baby," Eugene whispered, sending a message to Fritz through the roof's white upholstery.

Eugene pulled himself up from the floor and backed out of the open door. "Listen here, Mona. You deal with me or I'll leave you where I found you and somebody else can help you out of this mess. Got it?"

He leaned against the car door, giving Mona time, and the night of his own beating came in to his mind. Over two years ago, but still the fear paralyzed him. Men appeared out of nowhere, circling his Yellow Cab, their faces dancing furiously with pinched resentment. They yanked him from the cab with the help of his passenger and trapped him against a pastel blue house. The house was lit from the inside and Eugene saw a young white boy part the curtains, his eyes blank and unfeeling. Sick with anticipation and terror, Eugene burst through an opening between two men, trying to make it to his cab. One of the men, his face red and pockmarked, gritted his teeth at Eugene as he passed. A moment later, Eugene felt warm blood coursing down his neck. The man had sliced his cheek from behind. Eugene thought he was in the clear, but there was a blast, a dull thud reverberating through his leg. It was a brick, landing with the velocity of a tornado felling trees.

Mona opened her eyes, ready to fend off Eugene with a mean cringe, but when she saw his distressed face, she felt a part of herself crack. She wanted to cry. She wanted to let her tears answer him, explain her reluctance to trust him, but tears never changed anything for Mona. They hadn't stopped the men from coming into her room and emptying their hate into her body. The tears had not changed her mother. And they were of little help tonight, as Victor beat her to the ground with his fists and curses.

"Okay, I got it," Mona said, giving her defiance a rest. She tried to sit up but the sudden movement sent a sharp stab through her ribs. Mona looked up at Eugene, shocked and silent with fear.

"Oh no, I'm such a fool." Eugene moved back to the cab floor and saw her slip her hand inside her overalls. "It's your ribs, isn't it? Why didn't I check your ribs? Who was this bastard, Mona?"

The sobs leashed tightly to Mona's chest burst loose, sending a torrent of tears down her face.

"Hold on." Eugene kissed Mona's forehead and placed his hand over hers. "You're gonna be all right, you hear? We've got to go, Mona."

Between sobs, Mona nodded to Eugene, relieved he was taking over.

In moments they were speeding down an empty Lake Shore Drive. Mona quelled her tears and hummed as loud as she could, giving herself strength for what lay ahead.

CHAPTER THREE

COMETOTHEDOOR bounced against the bones of Rex's face. She slumped against the banister at the top of the stairs, her eyes red-rimmed, tight and puffy.

"Wake up, dammit, Eugene," she said aloud. "You're lucky I didn't come an hour ago," she grumbled, turning away from the door for the third time.

Rex needed to see Eugene. She had spent the night emptying a 1986 bottle of Tinto Velho, which left her irritable and stretching the limits of sleeplessness, but she had to talk to Eugene, to reconstruct last night, her father's words which kept running through her mind.

Dammit, she would get up if Eugene needed her: unwrap her arms from the warm body in her bed, pull back the heavy covers, slip her feet into her matted house slippers and come see who was at the door, knocking firmly, insistently. Couldn't Eugene sense it was her standing here, walking the halls?

Rex never wanted to get in the way of Eugene's life, nor did she want him to interfere with hers. He called himself gay now, so what was she? Straight, bisexual—asexual. Lately, she had spent more time lusting after the new silk being brought in from China than she did men, or women, for that matter. The last person she had touched was Eugene and that was for a hug and a dry peck on the lips. It had been ten months. Before long it would be twelve months, one lousy year, and she really wasn't trying to win any trophies.

Rex's well-worn red cowboy boot flew up from the floor and whooshed down on the bare wood floor. In response, pots and pans crashed in the apartment next door. A hissing "sheeet," followed by the scampering feet of a child echoed through the hall.

Maybe Eugene wasn't home. It didn't fit, though. Eugene was a homebody, liked his bed and would sleep on his ratty couch before lying in someone else's bed. He also liked to cook his own breakfast. He was the only man she knew who had three kinds of sausages at all times in his freezer, stores of Welch's frozen grape juice and a gallon apple juice bottle filled with grits—for easy pouring, he told her. Started his day right, he said. Rex operated on coffee until noon and rarely ate breakfast.

"Rex, that stuff isn't feeding your brain cells, it's eating them," he teased her.

Rex fingered the key to Eugene's apartment. She could let herself in. She imagined herself on the other side of the door, standing in the living room, looking towards Eugene's bedroom. She bit the inside of her cheek, pulling at the soft tissue. The thought of Eugene draped over a man was, well, unthinkable. In the bedroom, she saw herself standing over two moist bodies, limbs intertwined, one body indistinguishable from the other. The other man would get up from the bed, his erect penis taunting her, reminding her of her failure to satisfy Eugene. "Get out," he would insist. Eugene would lie there, his eyes lazy and noncommittal.

Rex dismissed the scenario. Eugene would never allow someone to ostracize her. He would never shame her. But she couldn't help feeling indignant. It was hard to accept these men Eugene claimed to be so in love with. Many of those she had met were arrogant and short towards her. Eugene had never had friends like that before. What was he looking for?

Rex missed Eugene. The security of him, his being there, right there, for her. And yet, he had moved on, why couldn't she?

She walked to the end of the hallway and stared out the window, across the street at the litter strewn against the curb. She wished for sleep, for a reprieve from the turmoil in her stomach, behind her eyes.

Dented beer cans lay against the curb like the body of a snake. Empty crumpled packs of cigarettes, balls of newspaper, popsicle sticks, blue crushed glass and city dirt filled in the multicolored scales. Rex recalled the significance of the snake from her dream book.

Health, regeneration, cycles. "Life, love, happiness—that's me," Rex mouthed sarcastically, laying her forehead against the pane. She thought she had found happiness with Eugene, but their marriage had ended after ten years. Years of struggling to create sexual intimacy where there was none, and the last two years pulling away from what was comfortable, convenient.

Rex closed her eyes and took a deep breath, letting the air fill her lungs. She expelled the breath slowly through her mouth, then repeated the cycle. With each exhalation, she whispered, "Doubt drains from me, leaving me whole and open." Breathe in, breathe out. She repeated the affirmation until she felt calm enough to open her eyes.

Rex walked determinedly back to Eugene's apartment. She pulled out her keys and unlocked the door, sticking her head through the opening.

"Eugene?" she shouted. Her voice rushed back to her unanswered.

She entered the apartment and stood in the living room. The green couch, a stereo cabinet and bookcase were tucked into the room next to the heavy table facing the window, which occupied an entire wall. The table was littered with newspapers, business cards, a stack of file folders, bills. Stones and shells lay in a large black ashtray between two empty silver candleholders, an oasis in the clutter.

Rex began a slow wade towards the bedroom. At the door she held her breath and peered into the cracked opening. The bed was empty and freshly made. The white comforter was tucked neatly to flatten its unruly swells. Granny Pinky's lime green and white pyramid-patterned quilt was folded at the base.

She pushed the door open and approached the low, glass-topped mahogany dresser. She was drawn to a photo in a black wooden frame of a man she didn't recognize. He had a moustache and wore small round spectacles. In jeans and t-shirt under a wool suit jacket, he aimed a camera towards the mouth of one of the Art Institute's lions.

"So this must be Fritz," Rex mused. "Wonder when I get to meet him." She replaced the photograph and picked up a picture of herself, taken when she and Eugene first met. They had gone to Georgia, vacationing outside of Atlanta. She had been surprised to discover a rich countryside where fall was more brilliant and exhilarating in its reds and oranges than anything she had experienced in Chicago. In the picture, her head was thrown back in laughter, her trench coat flapping in the wind, a blanket of crushed leaves beneath her feet. The faint woody smell of potpourri in a basket on the dresser took her back to that trip to Georgia, reminding her of the only time she could honestly say she had few doubts about the direction of her life.

Lastly, Rex picked up a photograph of Eugene's Granny Pinky. She was an old woman in the picture, sitting in a rocking chair, her hands crossed in her lap, head tilted to the right, smiling mischievously. Rex had met her only once, on that trip to Georgia. She had been welcoming, full of wry humor, pleased to see Eugene married.

Rex sat the picture down and reached for a bottle of Eugene's cologne. She thought to spray a bit of it on her wrists, but caught a glimpse of herself in the large mirror over the bureau. She quickly set it down again and left the bedroom, closing the door behind her. Stepping quickly through the living room, Rex let herself out, locking the deadbolt.

Outside the sky was soft, gray melting into blue. The humidity sat on the edge of the air, pushing at the coolness Rex drew into her lungs.

Rex sat on the top step of the building. She leaned forward, propping her elbows on her knees and dropped her head into her hands. She was disappointed that Eugene was not home, but more disappointed with herself, rummaging through Eugene's belongings. Maybe accepting Eugene's life was one thing and seeing him happy and in love with someone else—a man—was another challenge altogether. Eugene must suspect her uneasiness, he still hadn't introduced her to Fritz. She would have to deal with her insecurities. She wasn't going to lose her best friend over this.

Rex stared dully at the sidewalk. She believed she still had a right to Eugene's warm barrel chest, no matter who was in his bed. She could hear her girlfriends telling her to go find another chest to lay on. Her father would tell her to grow up.

The terrain of Eugene's chest was so unlike her father's, that last time she remembered laying against it as a girl. Her father's chest had never been completely open and vulnerable, but she never doubted his attention to her care. Still, there was something a child gets from its parents that she had been denied. She would have liked a large ceremonial nurturing from her father, rituals she could hold onto when she was feeling adrift. Her father was an oddity in his time, raising a child, a girl child, alone. But did that make it okay? She was always left wanting more from her father, so much more.

Rex wanted her life out where she could see it. As a copywriter, she was good at defining problems for others. But when she was the one with the problem, she was much less adept. Eugene had always been there, keeping her together through difficult times. They would talk, sometimes for hours, until the problem was defined, complete with an action plan. She needed to have that talk now.

Rex sighed, bending back the slight nail of her index finger with her teeth, and treaded back over the events of her sleepless night.

Her father arrived at her door early last night, his face a tense mask. Stepping through the screen door, he delivered two words, "Forgive me."

The words caused searing images to leap into Rex's eyes: burning hillsides, smoking houses, charred steel frames. The flames were scorching, red and golden, bigger than life.

He dropped his eyes before he swept the screen door back and walked out. Then he stopped, turning back towards Rex.

Their eyes met squarely as he kissed her on the forehead. "That's all I got to say, Rex," he said turning away, leaving Rex to find the missing chapters of his story.

Rex spent the rest of the evening sifting through ashes, dissecting the inflections of his voice. She replayed the particular rhythm of his words, his phrasing, his tone, the bass line. What she heard was a man caught between his past and the prospect of a bleak future. She had known for a long time that Otis was stuck in a corner, but she hadn't fully acknowledged all the signs of his imprisonment: the melancholy taking up permanent residence in his eyes, a fat man sitting square on top of each eyeball.

Rex spent years trying to coax her father into telling her the unadorned version of her mother's leaving. What if his appearance last night had something to do with that story? *Forgive me?* The words sped past her, tantalizing and terrifying. But when she marched the words back, stopping them within inches of her face, they had lost their size, become bland and amorphous. She needed a plan for how to save her father from this downward spiral and to finally get the truth about her mother.

Rex's father was a musician and a drinker. "I am a drinker," he would say. "I am not a drunk." Known to his friends as D, Otis Douglass Jr. made people laugh with jokes and twists of phrase. In private, the young girl would beg her father, "Daddy, tell me the truth. Tell me something straight, Daddy."

"I love ya, and I need ya, and I ain't never gonna let you go," he sang teasingly to his lanky nine-year-old daughter. Song lyrics he had written in the '50s when life, he said, was meaningful. He had been the front man. Played piano and sang his own songs. He was the local Billy Eckstein, the man with vocal cords wrapped in maple syrup. His ambition had been just big enough for this city—and not a mile beyond.

Those were times young Rex often tried to imagine: burgundy night skies, spacious lemon-yellow dance halls and pretty hazelnut-colored women in lowcut formals and high heels, who could cut a rug and weren't afraid to sweat. Now her father supported them with occasional gigs and by working for the Chicago Musical Instrument Company repairing instruments.

"I shoulda seen it coming. Your mama didn't like to sweat. That's how she walked off without you, Roxanne, cool as a cucumber in August."

"Tell me more, Daddy. Tell me about Mama."

"She was a gold pot of honey, a sweet drop of dew, legs to make ya wan—like—her, and—hmmm—that made you stew..." he sang, stumbling over the words too adult for his daughter. "But she didn't sweat. Uh uh. Not your mama. Damn, didn't see it."

"Did she like to sing too, Daddy?"

"Nope. Your mama couldn't hold a note."

"How did you meet her?"

"In a dark alley. Misty night. A full moon and the werewolves were stalking the dance hall. She's lucky I was a smoking man at the time. Went out to have a cigarette and found her there. A big hairy werewolf about to put his fangs through her neck."

"That's a vampire, Daddy," Rex said, exasperated. He told her the same stories, made-up tales which brought her no closer to the truth.

"Well, I saved her life. She was mighty grateful. Gave me little Roxanne as a gift to show her appreciation."

"That's not what happened," Rex said. "Tell me what happened, Daddy." She craved real stories about her mother, not Otis's fairy tales and fantasy characters.

"Close enough, Roxanne. That's close enough, sweet baby. Now you go on outside and play. Go on."

At nine Rex knew that her mama had "tits" and "ass." She'd heard these words when her father played cards with his musician buddies. She would be put to bed early and knew it was a card night when her father plugged in her nightlight and shut her door tightly. These were nights she made up stories, sometimes as many as ten before the men would arrive. They would take over storytelling then, supplying her with new words and ideas which she spent weeks deciphering. These were stories she never heard in school or read in the Nancy Drew books her father brought home with his last paycheck of the month.

"Tits" and "ass" were words that rang out more loudly than the others. She imagined her mother in the company of these men. Her father's songs and the excited pitch that accompanied the stories convinced Rex that her mother must have been a beautiful woman. Otis never brought other women into their house. Rex believed it was because he missed her mother. It meant that her mama was special, possessing something that made her wanted.

Rex often felt unwanted in this teasing house of men. She wondered what it would have felt like to be held by her mama, to crawl into her soft lap and lay her cheek on her mother's breasts. Lately, her father had stopped touching her. She longed for his touch, for the times when he swept her off the floor and pulled her to him. Rex had tested his new resolve against her, climbing into his lap after a fall from her bicycle. His thighs had become leveled rock, his chest, a frozen sheet of ice.

The smell of liquor would enter her bedroom as the card nights grew old and stale. Rex imagined the men's skin saturated with the alcohol they drank, gaseous fumes rising out of their bodies. The fumes would collect, dry ice floating down the hallway, seeping between the cracks in her door.

When she was thirteen, Otis Jr. sent Rex to an academy in Indianapolis. Rex never lived with her father again. She spent years living out of a suitcase. The academies, the summer camps were never home.

Rex stood up and looked down the block hoping to see Eugene's cab turn the corner. She craved coffee, the burst of energy caffeine would give her, craved it more than the sleep she needed. She started down the stairs, deciding to call in sick to work. A day at home would help clear the wine cloud in her head.

She walked to her 1967 metallic green Mustang. The street stretched its arms into the day. A car engine revved then sputtered. A news report and the buttery smell of baked biscuits descended from an open window. A couple approached her on the sidewalk, their gait as weary as her own. They reeked of the streets. Their clothes, stale with dry sweat, hung loosely from their gaunt bodies. Each carried an orange trash bag slung over their backs. They looked up as they passed, identical frowns pasted on their faces.

"Forgive you for what?" Rex muttered as she watched the couple shuffle down the block.

She unlocked her car and threw the door open. An unexpected rage burst from her and she caught it, cupping her hands over her mouth.

Swinging her long legs into the car and starting the ignition, she couldn't stop the words, spewing out like lava.

"Let me decide who's guilty," she said bitterly as she drove away from the curb. "I'm going to drag it out of you, old man. I want to know what happened back then. I want to know about my mama."

CHAPTER FOUR

One thousand one, one thousand two, one thousand—No Parking at Any Time. One thousand one, one thousand two—STOP; one thousand—Dr. Martin Luther King Jr. Drive. One thousand one, one thousand two, one thousand three—To 90/94. One thousand one—STOP.

Eugene drove down King Drive, coasting at the 35 mph speed limit. Mona sat stiffly in the passenger seat. She fixed her eyes straight ahead, counting the number of seconds it took the car to reach road signs and pass from her sight. As she shifted, her mind slid away to the part of her body registering pain.

My chest. My back. Below my ribs. I can hardly breathe. Mona descended into her right side until she was looking up at Victor's fists exploding onto her body. Why hadn't she moved, protected herself? She had huddled there like a helpless baby, her hands cradling her head, her right side totally exposed.

She had refused Victor again. But not until after he pulled her into his arms, close enough to smell his breath, moist and pungent like soil under winter leaves. She wanted all of him: his arms locked around her, his body pressed against her, his breath entering her.

The overalls collapsed like a parachute around her ankles. She stood covered only by her gray t-shirt hanging over her thighs. She was stunned by a sudden memory of herself, much younger, locked in a room with a man, afraid.

Victor began to lift her shirt over her head.

The man was familiar. He was hiding in a corner of her darkened room, waiting. Why?

Mona quickly caught the shirt with her elbows and covered her exposed body. For a moment she and Victor held each other's gaze, each deciding their next move. Mona looked away first, her eyes resting on a white wall reflecting the pink glow of the streetlight.

She pulled up her overalls, hooking only one strap. In the dark, she frantically looked for her things, soon realizing she had brought nothing with her. She knew Victor was angry. His eyes bore into her as she put on her shoes, desperately trying to put herself back together. She ran a checklist: Mona Elizabeth, fourteen years old, eighth grade, five foot two, ninety pounds, brown skin, brown freckles...

Victor stood near the door, his arms crossed over his chest. He was waiting for her to pass so he could catch her arm, snap her back to him. Who did she think she was, running away again, teasing him? When Mona slid along the wall, disgust flickering from her eyes as if he were a rodent, he let her go, slamming the door behind her. "You'll see, you silly bitch," he yelled as Mona ran down the stairs.

One thousand one, one thousand two, one thousand... Mona glanced at Eugene. His face was expressionless, his eyes nailed to the road. She remembered the look of deep concern he had held over her in the hospital.

Mona lay on the table waiting for the doctor. Her dried blood stuck to the flimsy paper gown. The nurse had given her a warm blanket, soothing against the cold hospital air. Eugene held her hand. He reached out for her in the moments when she would have asked, if she could have, but the whole situation was messed up and she wasn't talking. In X-ray, she concentrated on Eugene's strong hand in hers. She carried the comforting image with her now.

Mona shifted slightly in the seat and looked out the window, losing herself in the sunshine, shifting light over the surfaces of the passing signs.

Sunlight was a kind silence. Its brightness a warm cinnamon milk against her closed eyelids. It smelled of crushed violets and the faint scent of Dove soap hidden in her underwear drawer. The sunlight stimulated Mona's blood, her senses, her thoughts, and made her feel glaringly visible. She felt sick to her stomach, out of place in this daytime world.

Mona knew her face was a crime. There was a mirror behind the visor, but she was afraid to look. Her fingers told her that one eye was nearly closed, her nose swollen to twice its size. She grieved for her face, wanted to bury it: in the shadows under buildings, behind trash bins, down reeking garbage-strewn alleys. Her face belonged underground, where earthworms burrowed through muddy soil.

Mona slid her head outside the window, quickly, to avoid Eugene's reproach. Her face met the rush of humid air. The breeze swirled, building pressure against her cheek. A thousand prickly straight pins, then a warm anesthesia washed over her bruised face. The warmth turned to heat and soon her face was a burning coal. Mona imagined the window shattering inside the car door shell, pieces of glass lifting up, flying like fists to cut the planes of her face.

"Mona?" She heard Eugene's imploring voice. "Come back inside the car. Come on now." His voice was the train whistle from the night before, traveling away.

She was shattering. Like an ice cap she cracked, thrust into a million pieces. She wanted to let go. Let the pieces of herself fly. She pushed the thoughts harder to the left, to the side of her body where the pain was less, where there was room to hold more. She wanted to hide.

Mona recalled the looks they gave her at the hospital. The nurses. The policeman. The social worker. The doctor, examining her. Everyone whispering, their hooded eyes blaming her, damning her.

Now she was riding towards home where Ruth waited, collapsed in a chair, grinding her teeth, working up her anger.

"Mona?"

Eugene's voice was closing in. She pulled her head back into the car, careful to ease her right side gently into the cushioned seat.

"Mona, talk to me some," Eugene pleaded. "Where's your head at right now?"

Mona ignored him, returning to the passing road signs. One thousand one, one thousand two, one—her mind stalled. The maples edging Avalon Park, a block from their street, had come into view.

She inched her body towards the door, away from Eugene. Her thoughts were popcorn kernels over a hot fire. How would Ruth react to her black and blue face? She would slap Mona for being slapped. Her half-shut eye? Ruth would shut the other eye, spitting curses into it. Ruth would pick up the nearest half empty bottle of bourbon, light a cigarette and cry. Cry for her baby, but mostly for herself.

"You make me tired, Mona," Ruth would say. "You were a mistake." She would take her bottle and her cigarettes into her bedroom and shut the door.

Her Grandma May told Mona, "You try to love your mother. She's hard-headed, won't let go of the past, but you hold on to her. She's the only mama you got." Before her death, Grandma May and Ruth hardly spoke to each other. Mona never knew why. She struggled to love her mother, a bitter woman staring glassy-eyed at life through a bottle of booze.

The only time Mona recalled her mother extending herself beyond the walls of their apartment or the corner bar was when Ruth attended the Baptist church on the other side of the park. After three Sundays, Ruth invited some of the people she'd met over for a card party. She prepared little ham sandwiches, cutting the crust off the fluffy bread. She made a potato salad, cole slaw and baked beans. Ruth nursing a glass of sherry, stood over her as Mona made a relish tray.

When the guests arrived, Mona excused herself and went to watch TV in Ruth's bedroom. It didn't take long for Ruth to drink too much. Mona heard her mother's voice, sloshing around the living room for attention.

"When my baby sings, she sounds like an angel," Ruth said.

Mona turned the volume down, straining to hear, surprised her mother was saying something good about her.

"An angel with her head stuck in a hollow log," Ruth added, her cackles bouncing off the walls. "My water broke while I was taking a shower and, I'm telling you, Mona popped her head out for a little peek at the world. When they pulled her out of me, I'm not lying, that girl sounded waterlogged from the first holler."

Mona heard the nervous titters from the front room. She turned the television back up to extinguish her mother's voice. Mona stared into the screen, embarrassed by her mother's looseness and country manners. Grandma May, who lived her entire life in the country, might have told the same story, but she wouldn't fall all over herself, slurring her words, bellowing like a truck driver. Mona took the blanket from the back of the chair and wrapped it around her shoulders. She swallowed the rock hard feelings pushing their way up her throat, and set her face in stone.

Ruth felt her company pulling away. The card game dissolved into a jittery hush. She watched as they folded their cards and got up to fill their plates, ignoring her, making small talk in one corner of the room. What did she have to be ashamed of? She was raising Mona best she could. She put food on the table, brought home a paycheck from the post office for thirteen years. Who were they to judge her? Ruth drank the bourbon until it was gone, sinking deeper into herself. She half-heartedly offered to start a second round of Spades. Sitting at the card table, she beckoned to the fivesome to join her.

"Hey Marlon, Bobbie, Marie, come on over here. Who wants to go again? I'll pair up with one of y'all."

Ruth saw Marlon motion with his head towards the door.

They weren't willing to give her a chance? "Fine," Ruth said rising to her feet, the liquor fueling her anger, "you sanctimonious churchgoers. Love thy neighbor—kiss my ass."

"What did you say?" Bobbie screeched, her five-inch scarlet nails thrown over her heart.

"Get the hell out! That's what I said. Out of my house." Ruth collapsed onto the table, burying her head in her arms.

The guests scurried out, except for Johnnie. He came over and tried to apologize, but Ruth stuck her bony arm in the air and waved him out, the motion making her head spin. When she heard the door close, she waited a minute for the room to settle. She pushed herself up from the table then yelled at Mona to go to bed.

Ruth staggered into the kitchen, got a hammer from the drawer, took it to her bedroom and smashed in the television screen. She left a gaping green hole in the plastic cabinet.

Mona had a bruised kidney and a fractured rib. She met the social worker that morning in the Pediatric Ward where she was being kept for observation. "His name is Victor Owosu. He lives in that yellow building between Eighty-Third and Eighty-Fourth on Stony Island, number eleven."

"Did he rape you?" asked the the police officer, the rape counselor, the doctor. "No, *he* didn't," Mona insisted.

The doctor wanted to check between her legs. "Just in case," he said, with his false assurances and his big, hairy pink hands.

She hated his hands inside of her, exposing her, jamming into her with cold jarring metal.

"Victor was mad because I wouldn't have sex with him... No, I've never had sex with him...I don't know if she knows about him...He was mad, too, because he saw me talking to another boy from school...No! I told you. I never had sex with Victor..."

Well who? They wanted to know *who* she had sex with. Mona tried to tell them about the men, about the dresser she shoved against her door, but the words stuck in her throat. They blamed her. What business did she have with a thirty-year-old man, anyway?

A social worker had arranged to come to Mona's house to meet her mother and to take her to the police station when they picked up Victor. Her mother was going to hit the roof— bringing outsiders into their house.

"I can't go home," Mona said to Eugene. "I'm not going back there."

Eugene stopped the cab on a side street next to the park.

"Now Mona, I know it's been hard at home..." he started.

"You don't know," Mona shot at him, cutting her almond-shaped eyes. "What does anybody know about me?" She turned her head sharply towards the window.

"Okay, Mona, I'm sorry. You're right, I don't know. And I don't know where to take you. Or who would come after me when you don't show up at home. There are a lot of holes we've got to fill in here, Mona, and you have to help me out."

Mona considered Eugene, looked at her hands in her lap. She couldn't stay with him. She knew how people talked. Talked about Cabbie and his "men friends." "Did ya see that woman Cabbie was married to? Umumum, how'd he let a beauty like that get away? Man must be out of his mind." Ruth would never stand for that. She'd find her way across the street or call the police to come and drag Mona back home.

"Mona, are you listening to me, girl?" Eugene asked, interrupting Mona's thoughts.

"Yeah, I heard you. I can't go home with you."

"You think your mama's waiting?"

He was in no hurry to meet Ruth. Earlier, he had called Ruth to get her permission to release Mona from the hospital. She was drunk, pretty near incoherent. Afterwards the intaker called and Ruth gave her consent over the phone. Ruth told the intaker Eugene was her brother, Mona's uncle. Great, now he was part of the family.

"What time does your mother go to work?"

Mona faced Eugene. "She hasn't been going."

"Does she still have a job?"

"I don't know. She doesn't talk to me."

"She'll have something to say about this, won't she?"

"Yeah, she'll tell me she hates me—why don't you leave me alone."

He rocked towards her, using his hands to explain. "But Mona, honey, you need to be taken care of. Someone has to watch after you. The doctor said six weeks minimum for your rib. And your kidney..."

"And you think my mama's gonna be my nurse? Right. She can't take care of her own self. Don't worry, I can take care of myself—like always. I'm not going back there."

At first, Mona didn't know how to stop Ruth's "boy-friends" from coming into her bedroom. She avoided making the loud struggling noises that might awaken her mother, though she knew Ruth was passed out, her snores shaking the apartment walls. Mona could see that her mother had convinced herself that these men really cared about her. So if they slipped out of Ruth's arms to lay on top of Mona, didn't it mean that Mona was stealing the only love her mother had? Mona knew that underneath her mother's hardness was frailty, her pain ever-present in the tired valleys of her face, her alcohol-frayed nerves. She was afraid Ruth would throw her out or sink even deeper into her drinking spells, so Mona kept the trespasses to herself.

For a year, she awoke with men grappling and tearing at her, slobbering kisses on her face, thrusting curled fingers into her, pressing their hard sticks against her clenched thighs. Finally, she began barricading her bedroom door. Nightly she heaved her dresser full of clothes and linen across the room. The obstruction had stopped their attempts, but she didn't have the strength to move the dresser now. She never knew when the next man would show up banging at their apartment door, yelling Ruth's name, but wanting them both.

"Are you scared? Seems like you might have a few reasons to be scared."

"Scared of what?" Mona scoffed. "You don't know nothing."

"Mona. Listen, I can't take you home with me—everybody would know where you were anyway. You got any other people in the city you can stay with?" Eugene rested his lips on his fingers, pressed together as if he were praying.

"No!" Mona exploded, slamming her fists into her lap. A spasm of pain ran up her spine. She wanted to hit something, to stop him from asking her questions she couldn't answer, expecting her to come up with solutions she didn't have.

Eugene touched her shoulder. "Hey, you've got to go easy on yourself. We'll work something out. I promise. I'm not going to take you home if you don't want to go. Look at me, Mona. I won't take you there."

She put her head against the headrest and closed her eyes. Eugene looked into the rearview mirror, searching for options. Where could he take her where she would feel safe and he could have some time to think?

Maybe Rex...he could take her to Rex's. Eugene started the car. "We're going to Hyde Park. I've got a friend who will let us stay at her house until we can figure out what we're going to do." He slowly pulled away from the curb into traffic.

"Who lives there?" Mona asked, looking over at him.

"Rex—I mean, Roxanne. She'll be at work, but I have a key. We'll call her when we get there."

"Is that the woman who comes over? She's tight."

"What?"

"Tight. Cool. Dope...Um, she's what's happening."

"Oh," Eugene laughed at Mona's translation and her constantly changing moods. "Yes, that's her. That's Rex."

"You used to be married to her, right?"

"Yes, again. How come you know so much of my business?"

"I don't know. I just do. I know a lot."

"Hmm. Well, listen Mona, your mother's going to wonder where you are. We can't avoid her forever."

Mona knew her mother wouldn't wait for her all afternoon. If she wasn't down at the bar already, she was probably passed out, like she had been every afternoon lately.

"We've got a lot to think about. We'll go to Rex's for a few hours. We can get some sleep and eat some decent food. Then we'll put our heads together."

"Yeah, okay," Mona said, turning her body away from him. How long would Eugene stay with her? She would run away before she went back home.

"I promised you I wouldn't leave you, Mona."

Eugene put his attention on the road, worried that he was making promises he couldn't keep. An image of one young girl in Fritz's exhibit appeared in his mind. The girl was a little younger than Mona, her penetrating ebony eyes ringed black and blue. She held a brown stuffed doll whose yarn hair had been cut to nubs. The girl sucked her thumb, her eyes pleading for release from the hell in which she was living. The young girl reminded Eugene of Mona and he wished he could take her into his arms and rock her, shield her from her troubling life. He looked over at Mona. She had put her head out of the window again, her face turned to the sun.

One thousand one, one thousand two, one thousand three—STOP. One thousand one, one thousand two, one thousand three—STOP.

Eugene made a U-turn at 86th and headed back down King Drive.

Gloria Yamato

Don't Get Lost in the Translation

(Poems are excerpts from a larger work)

I. RHYTHMS

the rhythm of what was
is
the rhythm of what is   will be

according to some
it all began with
a Word

some folks say that
this all got started with
one glorious Big Bang

but everyone
seems to agree
that Time began

suddenly
in a flash!
in a flash!

in a flash in a flash in a flash!

the rhythm of what was
is the rhythm of what is
will be

and now look who's here

you and me
and it looks like we could
take ourselves out   just as suddenly

in
one
saythewordpushthebuttonpullthetriggerBigBang

FLASH!
in a flash!
in a flash in a flash in a flash in a flash!

the rhythm of what was
is the rhythm of what is will be

word has it
there are folks who couldn't
keep a beat in a bucket

I hear tell of folks who...well
rumor has it that rhythm
is about all they've got

we've all got a
heartbeat
the heartbeat

the pause   the pause
the heartbeat   the pause
the heartbeat   the pause

the stillness
of the dead
the going going gone

rhythms we are rhythms
all are rhythms are our rhythms

the rhythm of what was is

the rhythm of what is will be
rhythms are reminders
the stories of those who came before us

rhythms we are rhythms all
are rhythms   are our rhythms

I find myself thinking of those still to come

rhythms we are rhythms all
are rhythms   are our rhythms

the rhythm of what was
is the rhythm of
what is will be

the Ancestors   are asking
Have we heard them? Do we hear them?
Will we hear them? Can we hear them?

They are saying...? What are they saying?
They are saying...? What are they saying?
They are saying...? What are they saying?

what are they saying? what are they saying?

the rhythm of what was
is the rhythm of what is will be

the rhythm of what was
is the rhythm of what is will be

the Ancestors are saying
Omo

They are saying
Child

Don't Get Lost
They are saying
Don't get lost in the translation

V. NOMMO THE POWER OF NAMING

digging for roots of the family tree
searching for any sign of family history
I came upon a trail of names
Jenny Jackson
Jenny Smith
Jenny Threebits
Charlotte Jones
Charlotte Thomas
Charlotte Bennett

and one of them was me
the latest in a line of Jennies
that goes
all
the way
back to the boat
that's the way my family
speaks of the dead end to
the family tree
The Boat

my family calls me Jenny
after my grandmother Jenny
who was named for her grandmother
Jenny who was kidnapped
and brought from Africa on
The Boat

my niece Charlotte
was named for my mother

her grandmother Charlotte
who was named for her grandmother
Charlotte who came here on
The Boat
except that boat came from England
Jennies and Charlottes and Charlottes and
Jennies
generations interwoven
creating a new root system
for that big old banyan of a family tree

the first Jenny was African
the first Charlotte a Jew
both were women intent on doing
exactly what they set out to do

Jenny ran away from her captors right regular
well at least three times which is plenty
consider what was done to runaway slaves once
            caught
Jenny ran away
ran away
ran for freedom
run Jenny run   run Jenny run
run Jenny run Jenny run Jenny run
run Jenny run   run Jenny run
run Jenny run Jenny run Jenny run
run Jenny run   run Jenny run
run Jenny run Jenny run Jenny run
'cause who the hell wants to be a slave?
RUN

Jenny was probably making her last run away
            from
about the same time Charlotte came sailing into

The Deep South
according to her son   my grandfather
Charlotte proceeded to marry
the blackest man she could find
and was known to snap
when questioned about it
'the blacker the better
because black is what makes
you beautiful'

XI. AS BLACK CAN BE...

there are rhythms
so black, so Black,
black, Black
so Black and getting Blacker
at the speed of light

there are rhythms
moving fast fast
fast away from
assimilating

as black as beautiful can be
I'm the one
everyone once sought
to make mockery

now   I can't be
bothered
I am rhythm and symmetry
ready to just spread my wings

and fly high in this full moon   sky
black bird black as
rhythm and wonderful can be
I swoop and soar

towards the source
of a flash
it's my heart
of silver and gold
nearly stripped to the core

swoop to reclaim it
and up again
soar
high high higher
black bird black as genius
can be flying

genius can be flying
across the heavens
flying across the heavens
of my heart

FLYING!

FLYING!

FLYING!

YEAR OF THE NIGGER: 1959—1960

"Be good today, Pooky-Pooky-Poom-Poom-Pay." Mama kisses me gently on the cheek before she leaves me at the schoolyard gate. I stand blinking in the soft morning sunlight. Huge shadows spill across the playground. I see a classmate waving at me; I smile and walk towards her.

We can't play on the swings or seesaw without a grown-up to watch us. But we always find lots to do before the bell rings. Today, as more children arrive, the cold air mixes with our warm breaths, making magic. We become trains chugging, woo-woooo! We pretend to drink delicious hot cocoa, blow and slurp noisily at invisible cups. We puff on invisible cigarettes, scream then duck and run away from our own misty breath. Ghosts! someone yells. Scary witch fingers! someone else shouts. The game changes again and again.

One of the girls I am playing with says, "Why don't we run from the nigger?" Nigger. I'm not quite sure what the word means. It sounds like the word grown-ups at home use when something important is happening. "Nigga get down offa that before you fall down and break your fool neck." "Nigga, where you been? I ain't seen you in I-don't-know-how-long."

Wherever I've lived children don't say that word without getting in a lot of trouble. Maybe things are different here at William Lloyd Garrison Elementary, Boston.

Without missing a beat, I gulp the sweet cold air and scream out Niggers! with the rest. This reminds me of the game "Halp! Halp! God is coming!" I played that game last year when I was in kindergarten. Boy, did I get in a lot of trouble. You're not supposed to play with God.

I dash off with the pack of girls bellowing, "Aaaagh! Run! There's a nigger!" I love games where you run and scream and no one is really coming to hurt you. Only pretend.

I notice that every time the girl who made up the game looks back at me she screams, "Aaaagh! Nig-ger! Run for your life!" Her big gray eyes get even bigger. Her chestnut braids bounce and dance like streamers behind her. She looks so pretty! I scream too and stay right on her heels. I feel beautiful as we run like damsels-in-distress from the terrible nigger, which I imagine is green and purple and fifty feet tall. Oh! Who will save us?

We flit about the yard like a flock of chickadees twittering and shrilling at the top of our lungs. Suddenly the leader stops and turns on me. She stamps her foot and yells, "Why do *you* keep following us?"

I haven't been mean or said any bad words or done any of the things that mean, "You cannot play with us anymore!" Some of the other girls back away from me. Two of them have ugly smiles on their faces. They know something about this game that I do not.

Maybe if we start playing again, I'll figure it out. I run off a little ways. "Aaaagh! Niggers..." I try. A few of the girls are just as confused as I am. They run with me, eager to play again. The running keeps us warm. But the leader girl isn't playing.

"YOU can't run from the nigger, Stupid," she turns on me. "You are the nigger. We have to run from you!" From the looks on the girls' faces, I know that this is the part of the game I missed. Except, I still don't get how come I'm the nigger. I didn't say I would be "it." We didn't do eeny-meeny-miney-mo. Nothing! She just said, "Run!" and everybody did.

"I don't have to be the nigger if I don't want to!" I yell at her. "YOU be the nigger!"

"You are so a nigger, because that's what my mommy said you are! Only darkies like you are niggers. White people can't be niggers," she says in a sing-song whine like kids do when they think they are right.

She has not touched me, but I hurt like somebody smacked my face, punched me in the stomach and pushed me down all at the same time. I feel wobbly and sick inside. For some reason I think of my father teasing, "C'mon buddy, put up your dukes." That's when he wants me to take swings at his head while he dodges and laughs. He pokes at my belly. "If anybody picks on you, you gotta try to knock the hell out of them. Then come and tell me about it." Daddy doesn't like crybabies. Even though I want to pull that girl's hair and scratch her pink face, I can't. All of a sudden I get it. I get the game.

My Grandmama Taylor always tells me I'm her golden peacock. Daddy calls me Miss America. Do they say those things just so that I won't know that I'm a nigger? Maybe I'm a nigger for real. That girl's mommy said it and mommies know the truth.

But why wouldn't my mommy tell me! She always protects me. "Don't go any further than the end of the block so that I can see you from the window." "Don't talk back to grown-ups. People don't like sassy little girls, Vicky." Some of the things she tells me hurt my feelings. "No one else is going to tell you these things, but I will because I love you," she says.

I hear another little girl say, "You're really being mean and my mama said not to call anybody that."

The mean girl says, "Well, she is a nigger and my mama says I don't have to play with no little niggers. Ever!"

Their voices sing-song back and forth.

"Well, anyway I'd rather play with a nigger than play with you!"

"Nigger lover, nigger lover," some of the girls chant. They make a circle around the two of us when one girl takes my hand and tries to walk away. I won't move. I don't want to play with any of them. They're all little white ghosts, floating around me and I am a little brown statue who won't feel or play ever again. Everyone stares at me like I stared at the dead skunk on the way to school. Their eyes shine like bubbles. Their mouths make little circles. I hear the bell ring.

Someone tugs at my hand until I am standing in line. I feel cold from the inside out. It's snowing in my head. When the snow stops, I am sitting at my desk. Little kitten sounds push up from my chest and into my mouth. "Eeuuh...eeuuh," I whimper. I look out the tall beautiful windows, look out at the beautiful leaves falling from the trees. I look there to try and push the hurt away. But the teacher notices me.

"Victoria, you are not paying attention, are you?"

I try to talk but only the kitten sound will come out, "Eeuuh...eeuuh."

Miss Cohen walks to my desk and asks me what is wrong. I am afraid not to answer her, but I have forgotten how to talk. I can't look at her. Maybe she thinks I'm a nigger too.

"Are you sick? Do you want to go to the principal's office?" she asks.

I don't want to get into trouble. Maybe I will have to go to the principal's office for crying or for being a nigger. I don't know which is worse. My chest feels like a barrel with the straps around it too tight. I think I might burst.

My eyes fill with tears. They're going to overflow. I feel hot and dizzy. I can taste the oatmeal I ate for breakfast in my throat. I swallow hard. Cartoon music fills my head. I wish rubber ducks or plastic sailboats could sail down my cheeks instead of tears.

"Does anyone know what happened to Victoria?" Miss Cohen asks the class.

The girl who tried to help me on the playground raises her hand. "I know, Teacher! I know what happened!"

As she tells the story it is suddenly too much for me. Rough noises like barks and yelps pop out of me. Maybe I am a puppy, a kitten, a dead skunk. Not a little girl.

The room is silent except for the sounds I am making.

"Victoria, do you know what the word 'nigger' means?" the teacher asks. I don't want to have it explained to me again so I say that I do.

"What does it mean?"

"Colored people—like me." I cry even louder. My stomach feels like it is being pressed flat against my back. I am crying so hard that I begin to choke.

I expect Mrs. Cohen to point her finger at me and say, "You go the office right now!" Instead she leans down even closer. She wraps her arms around me like a blanket, almost picking me up out of my seat. And then I am crying and shaking so hard I feel like my baby sister Kelly's rattle. I'm afraid I might break into little pieces, but I can't stop.

Mrs. Cohen knows that I can read really good. So I feel special when we go together to look up the word "nigger" in the big dictionary. She keeps it by the window at the back of the class. Although my legs feel heavy, I nearly march to the dictionary like a soldier. Everything feels so important. No one can touch that book unless she says so. As far as I know, I am the first. She points to a word and asks me to read what it means to the whole class. The word seems to have too many letters to spell "nigger": N-I-G-G-A-R-D-L-Y. Because Mrs. Cohen has pointed to it, I believe that it spells "nigger." I believe the things grown-ups tell me. I read quiet in my head first to be sure it doesn't say something that will make me cry more. What if it says something bad about colored people?

"Go ahead, Victoria," she says. "Read it out loud."

As I read I feel all the sad feelings turning inside out. I know I'm going to be okay. What I read is, "Mean, small of heart, stingy." It doesn't say anything about colored people; it doesn't say anything about me.

"So," Mrs. Cohen says, "the real nigger is the person who called you that, and her mother, too!"

When I get over the shock of what Mrs. Cohen said, I see that everyone in class but me and the leader girl is giggling.

"I'm gonna tell my mommy!" howls the new class nigger.

"Well I certainly hope you do, young lady!"

Mrs. Cohen is really mad and catches the leader girl fast with her famous ear-twist grip and off they go to the principal's office.

Mrs. Cohen calls my parents and we learn that although she is white, other white people are bad to her because she is a JEW. Mrs. Cohen, like my father, believes in fighting back.

I don't hear that word "nigger" around my house much anymore. Sometimes, a grown-up will forget and start to use it but Mama looks at them out the corner of her eye like when she means business.

Grandmama Taylor still calls me her golden peacock and Daddy says I'm his Miss America. But it's not the same since that morning on the schoolyard and that girl with the bouncing chestnut braids.

"C'mon, put up your dukes buddy," Daddy teases. I swing for his head and for the first time, I don't miss.

MAIDEN VOYAGE

At eleven I am small for my age, but I swagger with the satisfying weight of more than a decade of living. I am the eldest child in my family, a position I take seriously.

For half the school year, I spend a groggy hour of each day riding across town to Jefferson Junior High, a school for gifted children. Our long trip is a small sacrifice for us colored children so advantageously tracked. A handful of our mothers patiently inch us through D.C.'s rush hour traffic.

In the beginning we are all friends. Willy exercises his ever-deepening baritone by singing R & B bass lines. He booms, "Duke, Duke, Duke, Duke of Earl, Duke, Duke, Duke of Earl..." until his mother's had enough. "Enough, Willy," she says firmly.

Willy is too deep into his song to catch the warning. "Nothing can stop me," he howls, "cause I'm the Duke of Er-er-er..."

Whack! Mrs. Richardson makes her point and Willy glares at his sister Pam and me as we snicker in the back seat.

Later, Willy and Pam double team me regularly. Their mother seals my fate by telling them to be more like me, "...such a little brain, so quiet." After a week of those remarks they both hate me.

Every afternoon as we wait, Pam and Willy taunt me mercilessly until their mother rounds the corner to take us home. I stick up for myself, but Willy is a husky kid and a natural bully; he counters my resistance by repeatedly punching me in the shoulder so hard my arm goes limp.

Eventually, I devise a plan to avoid the torturous rides to and from school. When my mother finally gets the story out of me, the ride arrangement is terminated. After she threatens, in no uncertain terms, to break their necks if they so much lay a finger on me, my contact with my tormentors dwindles to occasional rounds of tongue-spitting as they drive by.

My mother decides that at eleven I am old enough to catch the bus across town to school. She researches the route and before I negotiate it alone, rides with me once, making sure I know the landmarks that are the two transfer points on the three-bus trip.

I am anxious to take my first bus trip alone. I have to do it right. I want to get to school on time and I am eager to ride the bus with all the other screaming laughing kids. For days in advance I rehearse the trip, going over the routine in my head during spare moments, thinking about the stops I must be sure to look for, the number of blocks between one transfer point and the next.

The ride will take me through neighborhoods different from the row upon row of apartments in the Parklands where I live. My imagination races at the possibilities—ultramodern town houses and brownstones where I have to be ready for turf challenges by the kids who live there. I memorize everything. Then I mess it all up before I make it to a seat on the first leg of my trip.

Waiting at the bus stop on Monday morning, I am excited and awkward at once. Should I stand, silent and dignified, like the weary dark women in white uniforms? Should I read the newspaper like the gentleman enjoying a morning smoke? Should I play tag to keep warm with the other kids waiting with me?

When the bus arrives, I get on last so I can watch everyone and imitate their casual demeanor. I count my money again quickly. "It's fifty cents and don't forget to get a transfer," I remember my mother coaching. I watch the people ahead of me drop the change in the money box and hold their hands out for a transfer.

Tinkle, tinkle, clunk, the nickles, dimes and quarters tumble down the coin box. The driver hands out the transfers automatically. I drop my change in the box and wait for my transfer. And I wait for my transfer. And wait. Now everyone is seated and waiting too. The bus driver watches me impassively.

I don't know what to do. What have I done wrong? I quickly review the scene in my head, trying to determine where I missed a step. All I can figure is that the bus should be moving with me clutching my transfer by now.

I hold my hand out tentatively. Maybe I didn't hold my hand high enough for the driver to see. He notices it for sure now and he still doesn't move. Maybe he thinks I'm lazy. Maybe he thinks I'm a lazy colored kid.

But I'm not lazy. I help my parents with my sisters and brother. I never have to be told to do my chores and I do my homework—before dinner. The driver doesn't know this about me. Maybe he wants me to show him that I'm not lazy, always expecting someone to do things for me I can do for myself. Perhaps he's waiting for me to tear off the transfer myself. They're within my reach, closer, in fact, to me than they are to him. I wish he would say, "Help yourself," or even, "Get it yourself."

I reach for the transfer and POW! before I can blink, he slaps me, slaps my hand hard hard hard. He could have slapped my soul for all the dread I feel. He starts yelling at me, and I am ashamed, a disgrace to my race. What will I do now?

No one on the bus moves. No one makes a sound, not even a cough or chuckle. My nose itches but I can't move my hand to scratch it. People are looking out the windows or straight ahead, but not at me.

"What the hell do you think you're doing...who the hell do you people think you are?"

I know who I am but I don't respond; I can tell he doesn't want me to say anything. I am afraid to say anything. What if he throws me off the bus and I'm late for school?

His pale face reddens. "I am sick and tired of you colored kids! Can you say 'please'? Hasn't anyone ever taught you any damn manners..."

I think how simple it might have been if I had known what he wanted. "What would you like," he might have asked. "I would like a transfer, please and thank you," I would have answered. My parents taught me these things. I like these polite little rituals.

"Transfer, please," I say softly as he continues to rant.

"What?" he says.

"Transfer, please," I repeat.

My hand is stinging, cheeks are burning. Every moment I stand here costs me pride. I ignore the deep ache welling inside my chest.

The driver looks away, the wind suddenly gone from his sails. Does he imagine I will disappear? I am still standing there when he looks back at me. He rips a transfer off the narrow pad and hands it roughly to me.

"Thank you," I say, anxious to ward off further attack.

"Go sit down and don't you ever do that again," he chastises as he pulls the bus away from the curb.

I force myself to walk towards the seats, avoiding the eyes of the passengers who look away as I pass. I drop stiffly into the first vacant seat, the transfer sticky in my sweaty palm. I am sitting next to a black woman about my grandmother's age. I can tell she is angry, her body is hard as stone next to mine. I believe she is angry with the driver until she rolls her eyes and glares at me.

"You got exactly what you deserved," she hisses.

I do not respond but instead watch my fingers uncrumple the transfer, smoothing it out against my leg. I try hard not to think about the bus driver or the way I feel. I try hard not to think about the woman next to me. I am afraid if I look up, everyone will be staring at me.

A while later another black woman gently touches my shoulder as she passes by my seat.

"Honey, be sure you tell your mama exactly what happened," she said. "Tell her everything," she added, shaking her head as she stepped off the bus.

PHARANG DAHM!

She was always being rubbed the wrong way. The constant aggravation left Neva emotionally raw. White people. The anger she had fought off for so long slammed hard into her. It intensified with the heat wave that caught everyone off guard.

100 degrees. In Seattle, temperatures above 60 degrees resulted in outbreaks of "sunfluenza." All who were able beat a hasty path to the nearest "beach," as the grassy areas near any available body of water were called.

Neva tossed her way through each sweat-laden night, her sleep crowded with endless streams of white light, white people, white noise that always led back to the jagged scar filled with crooked teeth. Then came the scornful twanging of his voice, the doggish words that bit into her dreams and shook them until they were ragged.

"Y'all cain't come in here."

"You bettah teach that little nigger some manners."

Neva flapped, kicked and thrashed her way back to consciousness. She awoke shaken. Her fingers and toes curled back for a full yawn and stretch. Finally, her body trembled with a welcome surge of energy. Once again it was time to navigate, time to plot routes that would take her to those passages where the mainstream was narrowest, shallowest. Neva imagined bobbing on the waves of her anger instead of being pulled under. Pharang Dahm! Black foreigner.

This week Neva relied on Zap Mama to help keep her attitude in check. She punched the "play" button on the tape deck and rolled out of bed to the sounds of their good-natured chant.

"Got t'think positive, got t'think positive, got t'think positive...ah brrrru-oh-woh!"

"Oooooh! He makes me so angry," Miss Boo screeched at her TV audience. "Maybe I'll turn him into..." she thought for a moment, "...a TOAD! What do you say, boys and girls?" Miss Boo stirred her cauldron hopefully, as if she were really waiting for an answer.

"Let'm have it, Miss Boo," Neva screamed, eager to help her mentor out. Neva, perched on a chair in the middle of the kitchen, stirred her own witchy brew of ketchup, milk, salt, pepper and jam in Grandma Edith's big yellow mixing bowl. Baby witch in training.

Neva was an only child. Nothing her relatives could give her was denied. But under the influence of television and nursery school Neva's world and desires broadened. Her response to the inevitable "no" was to raise her voice, shrieking, indignant. Tantrums seldom got her what she wanted. Like as not, her grandparents laughed and held her parents at bay as she spun around on the floor. Neva's noise was tolerated as long as it didn't go on too long. One particularly warm summer night, that changed.

"Y'all cain't come in here."

Neva's immediate protest was quickly but gently muffled by Grandmama Edith's hand. A man at the entrance of the new amusement park she had pestered her folks to take her to was turning them away. As she flapped and screamed against her grandmother's grip in the back seat of their car, she heard her murmur, "Hush Baby, go to sleep now."

Go to sleep! That made no sense to Neva. She was wide awake, ready to ride the huge ferris wheel that would take her the closest she had ever been to the sky, the carousel where she would go around and around until she was dizzy. Her grandfather, Big Jim, had promised to win her one of the huge stuffed animals she'd seen on the television commercials. And her grandmother was telling her to go to sleep!

Accustomed to the ways of Jim Crow Georgia, they had packed their own sweets and refreshments, fried chicken sandwiches, potato salad, ice-cold soda pop and still-warm peach cobbler. They were turned away at the gate. NO COLORED ALLOWED.

"Oh, I'm sorry, suh. We misunderstood," Big Jim said to the pale-faced man at the gate. Big Jim's reply was the one everyone expected under such circumstances. It was contradicted only by Neva's scream from the back seat, the shriek of a child who "don't know any better, suh."

To Neva the man's mouth was a gaping wound with brown ragged teeth. A thin crooked gash across the lower part of his face. No lips. As he peered into their car, he screwed up his face as if he smelled something bad. He turned away from the window and spit out a thick wad of chewing tobacco.

"You bettah teach that little nigger some manners."

Neva heard him through the quilt her grandmother had pushed her under and now firmly held over her head.

"Shhh, Baby, go to sleep now," Edith crooned over and over, restraining Neva's thrashing as best she could. To Neva the world had fallen down and gone crazy-legged ever since.

Let's do it right today, Neva thought as she left her apartment. She set out early to avoid the heat and crowds on her way to the university. In the heat, Neva felt more vulnerable than usual, more likely to react without thinking. She could barely stand jostling against her lover, let alone the sweaty smelly bodies of strangers.

Neva lived in the Central Area of Seattle, the CD as it was called by the people who lived there. Many paths crossed as people made their way through the CD to other places. Black teens, moody with adolescence, flopped down onto bus seats next to white yuppies. Southeast Asian and Ethiopian newcomers, Native and Latino old-timers rolled down Beacon Hill through the CD. Sometimes the chemistry between all this difference was wonderful. Often the alchemy was lost to the explosive violence of stereotypes grinding noisily against each other. Neva knew in hot weather she slipped too easily into being evil to risk getting caught in a crush.

As she stood at the bus stop, Neva opened her umbrella to ward off the sun. Her great-aunt Eddie Dean had always carried an umbrella on her long walks through the hot Georgia countryside, young Neva trailing like a baby duckling, her tiny umbrella raised over her head. But it was in Thailand that Neva had learned to carry an umbrella regardless of the weather. During monsoon season, it was shelter against the pounding sun; later the same day it had protected her against the brief but scouring rain showers. But in Seattle, she walked across asphalt and concrete, not the dusty tree-lined roads of Udorn.

Neva thought she would ask the young woman waiting at the stop to join her under her umbrella, but the woman was making an obvious effort to ignore her. She kept her back to Neva, feigning distraction, pacing nervously. Neva closed her umbrella and squeezed into the narrow shadow cast by the bus stop shelter, stowing away her memories of Thailand.

Neva thought about skipping her classes and heading to Denny Blaine Park, once her favorite beach. Sal had introduced her to Denny Blaine a couple of years ago. She had met Sal in a modern dance class. A few weeks into the class Neva had forgotten herself, allowing the rhythm of the pulsating drum music to get under her wings. Like thermal currents the rhythm carried her up and up until she was soaring, circling, coasting on air. Suddenly, the jagged wound opened, bloodless and filled with teeth.

"Some of you have *too* much rhythm." The instructor criticized, her eyes following Neva as she crossed the floor. "I don't want rhythm, I want you to just feel the music, be loose, move freely." She motioned with her thin frame to illustrate.

"Maybe you can do both at the same time," Neva responded smoothly.

Beneath her bravado, Neva cringed. Her wings collapsed as she staggered and stumbled across the floor crashing into a corner. She cursed under her breath, quickly tucking away thoughts of feather and flight. She flattened her wings under her shoulder blades and pressed them around her heart, down into the small of her back.

"Don't let that cow get to you. She's full of it." The woman, Sal, looked as if she had been sprinkled with paprika. She didn't seem to care that the instructor could hear her comments.

Neva immediately warmed to Sal. As they became friends, Sal and Neva focused on their similarities, their love for dance and music, their passion for books and travel. They had an unspoken agreement to respect their differences. Neva was black, Sal was white. Neva was straight and Sal a lesbian.

In the end, Neva had wanted nothing to do with Sal.

"Hey Sal! Guess what?" Neva ran up to Sal's doorstep, panting.

"What?"

"I just figured it out. Everyone else probably knows already. Don't know how it got by me. Hah!" Neva lost control to a spell of snickers and giggles.

"What? What?" Sal asked, dragging Neva inside.

"Sal, I'm gay! I'm a dyke! Come on, let's go to breakfast and celebrate," she said, grabbing Sal in a big hug.

Sal winced, pulling away from Neva's grip.

"Jeez. I'm really sorry. I don't know what to say Neva. God. Life just gets harder. You're black, a struggling artist and now this."

Neva had never viewed her life circumstances in such bleak terms.

Later Sal confessed to feeling abandoned. "You were my only black straight woman friend. You gave me hope for the rest of the black community."

The fragile trust they had built suddenly fell away in big flakes.

"What! Are you kidding me?" Neva challenged.

"No, no," Sal stammered. "Don't get me wrong, Neva. I really admire you for being able to withstand all the oppression. You're just so strong."

Once Neva began dropping accommodation out of her socializing, the circles of her community grew smaller. Graciousness replaced gratitude. Confrontation replaced everything else.

Neva still went to Denny Blaine to play. "Dyke-kiki," as it was fondly named by local lesbians. Dyke-kiki, where she flirted openly or exchanged deep kisses with her girlfriend. Their idyll abruptly ended when local hets and tourists learned of the women's haven via the evening news and came to the beach to ogle. Some even tried to take pictures.

An anonymous dyke had broken the silence of the lesbians who sat defiantly if uncomfortably under the curious stares. Broadsides signed "Anon" appeared, slipped under windshield wipers and tossed through open windows. Anon focused her anger on the young black men who came to stare and jeer at "the ladies." More than once Neva returned to her car to find poetry protesting the threat of "young dark beasts boasting huge dicks" slipped under her wiper. One of the poems likened them to gorillas. King Kong and Fay Raye all over again. Pharang Dahm! all.

No one complained about the slices of middle-class white America. Red-faced men with protruding beer bellies and their prim and proper wives turned out to gawk in greater numbers, often bringing their children along to have a better look at the "perverts."

Neva had wanted to cram a broadside down the throat of the nearest person regardless of their race or sexual orientation. She had often dealt with the jeering and offhand comments of the young men who could have easily been her brothers or cousins. There were times when she wanted to hurt them as much as they hurt her.

It wasn't until she lived in Thailand that Neva had begun to watch people with little or no judgment. In Udorn, people stopped and stared when she walked by. At first it frightened and annoyed her to be so scrutinized. She remembered too vividly the stares she got when she shopped in mostly white stores in the States. The salespeople never took their eyes off her, as if waiting for her to steal something.

Once, sitting alone one afternoon in a Udorn café, Neva noticed a woman and man across the room. The woman stared at her intently. Neva's uneasiness grew to alarm when the woman suddenly leaned over and whispered to her companion, keeping a sober eye trained on Neva.

Images of a "Thai haircut" floated into Neva's consciousness. She had once overheard a young Thai man threaten a GI, apparently upset with his ugly American attitude.

"You better look out. Maybe you have Thai haircut," he warned.

For fifteen U.S. dollars, sometimes less, you could put anyone out of business—forever—with a "haircut" that started at the throat.

Neva couldn't imagine what she could have done to earn such punishment. She worried her ignorance of some local custom might have earned her a good thrashing. Was she sitting with her feet pointed towards them? She tapped her toes together to make sure, as that would be a grave insult.

The woman's companion stood and walked towards Neva's table. The blood rushed to Neva's face and quickly drained as he approached. Neva stopped breathing when the man, now standing over her, bent down.

"My friend say she like you face. She say you have a nice face. She like to look at you face."

The woman nodded at Neva and smiled. Neva managed a nervous chuckle.

In Thailand staring was not considered rude. The Thai thought it natural to look at people and things that appealed to them. After a few months, she became accustomed to the stares. "Su-ay, su-ay mak-mak." "Beautiful, how very beautiful."

Neva's experiences in Udorn had such an impact on her that when she reluctantly returned to the States, or "The World" as homesick GIs called it, people constantly asked her, "So, what country are you from?"

Muscles tense from tucking in her full lips, muscles tense from trying to hide her protruding butt, relaxed. It was ironic that when she wore her blackness most confidently, carried her body with grace, she was perceived as foreign by Americans, black and white.

"She'll just have to learn." Grandmama Edith's tone had frightened Neva. It was the same one she had used when Uncle Jim died. In the days after the scene at the amusement park, Neva's wailing resistance had eventually dissolved into a lingering sullenness that struck her family as a bad sign for someone so young.

The stories her elders recounted terrified Neva. It was grown-up business, but they didn't send her from the room as they had in the past. For the first time, she heard her relatives talk about white people. They talked about white folk refusing to serve colored people in public businesses. Less frequently they told stories of how colored people fought back. They rarely laughed. They fussed and hummed in frustration and grief. They sucked their teeth in disgust. Sometimes the women wept quietly, while the men sat with their heads bowed, their shoulders slumped.

But it was the stories about the lynchings, the images of broken, burned, colored bodies, that caused Neva to dream nightly of a man's screaming head burning in their fireplace. One night the head was Uncle Jim's. Neva ran sobbing from her bedroom, refusing to sleep alone for an entire month. It seemed there was no end to the horror that happened to colored people, people like her, who had been impatient, impertinent or just plain unfortunate. Every day there were new lessons. Neva was free to spread her wings at home, but the stories killed her desire to fly. One evening Neva calmly walked to her favorite corner in the den and laid down, folding her arms across her chest and shutting her eyes tight.

"Neva, oh Geneva," her grandmother teased, "What you up to now Miss Fancy?"

"Shhh! I'm dead," Neva whispered. "I'm waiting for God to come and get me 'cause I don't want to be here anymore."

No amount of coaxing would budge her. Perplexed, her family left her alone. After a half hour, God had failed to come for her and Neva fell asleep. When she woke up, it was with a small sting of dread that she experienced every waking thereafter. Of course God didn't take her. From the pictures she had seen in church and on the walls in her very own house, God was white and probably didn't want her in heaven. Since then, Neva approached white people with caution until she could fly across the waters, not to Guinee, as some of her ancestors had prayed, but to Southeast Asia.

"Hey! Neighbor! I know you in there!"

A few weeks after she had arrived in Thailand, Neva was startled by a loud impatient rapping at the door of her bungalow. As Neva walked shyly towards the door, the woman caught sight of her and smiled.

"Hey, there you are! I'm Lam. What you name?" the woman asked good-naturedly. "Oooooi! You don't come outta this bungalow soon, I gonna be more black than you!"

Lam held up her slender arm and pretended to gloat over her smooth bronze complexion. Her gentle joking manner made her a favorite in the compound.

"I can't speak Thai and I didn't think anyone here spoke English..." Neva apologized. She had exiled herself in the bungalow for more than a month, frightened of looking foolish or offending anyone with her broken Thai or American manner. She had insisted they live among the Thai, over her young Air Force husband's objections. Neva spent most of her mornings close to her open door, listening to the women in the compound talking among themselves as they passed by.

"You know you can't stay in here alla taam," Lam teased, peering through the screen. "Everybody wanna know when you gonna come out."

Lam not only spoke English but she was also an excellent mimic. One of her great pleasures was singing Japanese traditional and popular music. She entertained herself and anyone around by singing excellent renditions of Japanese favorites, complete with the gestures of the well-known stars who sang them. Neva felt fortunate to have found someone near her age who was as smart and outgoing as Lam.

"How old do you think I am?" Lam asked Neva.

They were sitting on Lam's porch waiting out the afternoon heat, playing gin rummy.

Neva knew that Lam was about to have one of those last-word moments with her. Neva had thrown her cards down in disgust when Lam guessed everyone's hand and then needled them to give her the cards she needed.

"Lam, you must've been playin' cards since you was a baby," Neva grumped.

Lam's challenge to Neva aroused the women's sagging interest. Oi winked at Neva as if she knew what came next. The women did not attempt to hide their amusement, accustomed as they were to Lam's ways.

Neva thought Lam was older than she looked. She figured white Americans had underestimated Lam's age, and that Lam likely associated their mistake with Americanness, rather than whiteness. This would be tricky. Lam had an easy friendliness and reckless confidence that Neva had attributed to youth. She had assumed that they were close in age. Now, looking into her smiling eyes, Neva could tell that Lam was older—much older than twenty-two—wiser and wilier than she had thought. She hoped Lam would not take offense and she wanted to be one of the lucky few who had the last word with Lam.

"Well, Lam, up until a minute ago I would have guessed you were my age," Neva drawled, studying Lam's face for a clue.

Lam smiled, nodding her encouragement. "So, go ahead. How old?"

"Thirty," Neva guessed. She figured Lam to be about twenty-eight but added a couple of years to be safe.

Lam's eyes widened. Neva worked hard not to let her smug satisfaction surface, as she leaned back in her chair. She was pretty good at feeling people out.

Lam looked thoughtful for a moment. Someone at the table whistled softly.

"I'm forty-two," Lam announced.

Neva's jaw dropped.

"Hah! Bettah shut you mouth before something fly in there," Lam crowed.

Neva laughed with everyone else. No tucking or stooping or holding back, but laughing, full out.

On campus, expanses of grass, bright green in the sunlight, ran emerald in the shade. Neva headed for the cool depths. She longed to take out her umbrella, especially as she headed into the exposed plain of brick plaza, "The Red Square," stretching endlessly into the harsh sunlight. Neva eyed the buildings surrounding the plaza, mapping out a route that would take her through their air-conditioned interiors and out onto 15th Avenue.

As she waited for her bus, Neva ducked into the promised coolness of a secondhand clothing shop. She listlessly poked through the old lace and linen, the tweed and musty denim. She recalled the stories passed down by her relatives of work washing and ironing the clothes of white people who took such "help," as their work was called, for granted. She remembered Grandma Fanny's dismay at having to work for people "with nasty attitudes and even nastier grooming habits."

Neva's head began to swim in the stifling closeness, the rank smell of old clothes, the collective funk of hundreds of bodies. The one small fan in the store only whipped the sluggish air and stink around. The heat in the shop swelled, bubbling up from Neva's belly and climbing, until beads of sweat popped out on her forehead. Her throat tightened and her stomach churned ominously. Neva fled from the store into the sunlight, filling her lungs with great gulps of humid air.

She quickly boarded the bus, disappointed that the only provision for cool air was two tiny fans mounted to the dashboard. Their concerted whinings gave the bus driver little comfort, and despite the open windows, the passengers slumped dispassionately in the sticky vinyl seats. The smell of decaying garbage wafted in and mingled with the odors of the perspiring bodies. Neva found a seat in the back and closed her eyes, leaning against an open window. A rolling breeze lapped at her neck as the bus gained speed.

Neva slipped into a heat-soaked sleep. Going home. Just over the hill. Or was it the place across the water? Her Thai friends called her Black foreigner, Pharang Dahm! but she felt more at home there than she would ever feel here.

If she were in Udorn she might be riding to market with Lam, drowsing in the midday heat as their samlar driver wound his way through Udorn. Dlaat! The open air market where the smell of roasting meat made her mouth water, where the smell of dried squid made her dry heave. Stalls of pots and knives gleaming silver. Brightly colored fruit and vegetables sold alongside equally colorful sandals and bolts of fabric. And the people. So many shades of brown. She might feel whole and in control of her life if she could remember everything she had learned between Thailand and Georgia.

Neva dreamt that she and Lam were walking down the road towards home, Neva's umbrella full sail. Lam walked beside her, singing a new Japanese song. As she had done a hundred times, she moved under the umbrella with Neva, putting her arm around her waist, resting her head on Neva's shoulder.

Home. Pharang Dahm! Pharang Dahm!

Rabie Harris

Diary of a Journey

The Lord is my Shepherd I shall not want. About ten years ago I started reading my Bible every morning. I would get up and, before I put in my teeth (I kept them in water in a small blue container on my night table), I would sit on the floor, lean my back against my bed and read. I felt very humble and religious, like a woman who wanted to do better with her life, feel good about herself. I will admit my mind often wandered. While I was reading, I would remember that my son, Henry, might stop by for breakfast before he went to work. I enjoyed fixing breakfast for him. Sometimes I would remember that snails had gotten to my squash. There was always something to think about.

I like to read the Twenty-Third Psalm—"The Lord is my Shepherd, I shall not want." I want to feel that God is with me and that I have no fears or wants. But I do. I want not to be here, in this house, and I want my husband, John, not to be gone.

Today is my first day in this place, and I have decided to keep a record. My youngest daughter, Karen, used to keep a diary. I read a few pages one day. She came in her room and saw me. She had such a look on her face. Before she could say anything, I said, "Your room is a mess. You should spend more time on your school work instead of all these boys you're writing about." I never saw the diary again.

My mind is filled with old times, but the children tell me my memory is not what it used to be. One doctor called my condition dementia; another said I was in the early stages of Alzheimer's disease. I have noticed a change in the quickness of my thoughts, but all in all I am fine. God willing, I'm going to continue writing as long as I'm able.

When my children look at me, especially my son, Henry, I can see that they are confused. They think I'm in a different world. Sometimes I feel that way too. I am trying to understand what's happening to me. Maybe Karen or one of the other children will read my diary after I am gone and they'll understand. I won't mind.

My daughter Diane brought me here with two suitcases. I used to have drawers and closets filled with clothes. I have lost so much weight that half my clothes don't fit me.

Mrs. Oliver, the woman who will be taking care of me, seems all right. Still, Diane was reluctant to leave me. She reminds me so much of myself, all feelings and not much brains, but I was not as serious as she is when I was her age. If she doesn't die from worries, she will die from gloom.

I try not to think about death. I've always been afraid of dying, more so after seeing John die. When I watched him gasping for breath, it was as if death had a life of its own and was taking my John's. I felt helpless as I watched his eyes blink and the odd smile that came across his face when he knew it was the end. I used to do everything for John, but I couldn't do anything to keep him with me. One second I had a husband; the next he was gone.

I have tended to the dead—my sister Myrtle. I remember plain as day when she died. John and I had been married seven years. It was early morning and we were asleep. A loud banging woke us up, and John went to the door.

Adam, the young man who worked with my sister in her small shop, asked, "Mrs. Nelson awake?"

I got up and went to the door and stood behind John.

"Mrs. Nelson, Myrtle dead. She drown," he said.

I washed her body and dressed her. I loved Myrtle, and I loved John, but when John died, I couldn't touch him. After forty years of marriage, I should pray to join him, but I don't. I couldn't stand knowing when I am to die, yet I think that if death came suddenly or in my sleep, I would know. It is that knowing moment that I can't face.

Diane talked to Mrs. Oliver about my diet and medication. She asked her to watch me carefully since I like to walk around. I have five bottles of medicine: for my heart, my stool, one to counteract the heart medicine, liquid multivitamins and Mellaril, a tranquilizer. I would never have swallowed so many chemicals when I was a young woman. I started taking high blood pressure medicine a few years back, but my pressure is fine now. As a matter of fact it's sometimes very low. I don't understand how a person like me who has watched her diet so religiously could be deteriorating at my age. The neurologist said that my condition might be hereditary. That shows how little control we have over our lives. Is this what my children have to look forward to?

I ate lots of fish, chicken and vegetables all my life. When my oldest daughter, Sandra, told me about cholesterol, I cut back on butter and the number of eggs I gave to John, even though I thought she was making too much about something I never heard of anybody ever dying from in Jamaica. Our friend, Mr. Miller, lived past ninety, and he ate eggs every day. I drank cerase tea to help clean my blood. Jamaicans swear by cerase. I bought a juicer and made celery, carrot and turnip juice. I went to bed at a decent hour, and I only drank champagne on special occasions. I did drink white rum, but that doesn't count since I used it as a medicine to put in coffee or teas for fevers and colds. After all my caution, I am here, sick.

Mrs. Oliver appears to be a stern organized woman. At one o'clock she came over to my chair and shook my shoulder lightly. I had just begun to doze off. I felt as if I was back in Queens, in my house—but I don't have that place anymore.

"Time for lunch, Mrs. Nelson," she said.

I looked up and for a moment she looked like an old friend, Mrs. Berry. Once, I got lost trying to visit Mrs. Berry. I fell asleep on the train and woke up at a station in the Bronx. I had walked three blocks before I realized I wasn't in Brooklyn.

Mrs. Oliver gave me a pork chop, beans, collard greens and corn bread. Small squares of fat were mixed in with the greens. I'm not supposed to eat that stuff. Surely Mrs. Oliver hadn't heard my daughter. I picked up my fork but couldn't put anything into my mouth.

"Mrs. Nelson, you have to eat. You want me to feed you?" Mrs. Oliver asked.

"I'm not that far gone. Thank you."

"Then eat or I feed you."

What is an old woman to do. I only had one mother, and God knows she was too much for me. I don't want anybody telling me what to do, so I will do what I must. I ate the greens first. They were very good, a little greasy. Grease makes me belch more than I usually do. The pork chop was so hard I had to tear it with my teeth.

After lunch I was very sleepy. I sat down in a recliner close to the front door where I could hear what was happening outside. I didn't know that I had fallen asleep, but I found myself in Sandra's house in Long Island. I saw her oldest girl, Mary, but she was just a little girl. She held one of the storybooks I had bought her. She tore and scattered the pages all over her mother's red carpet.

"Stop it, Mary," I scolded.

I offered to help her clean up, and we began picking up the pieces of paper, but when I took a good look at Mary kneeling beside me, she was Mrs. Oliver.

"Mrs. Nelson, you must have been some housekeeper. You've been cleaning up my carpet really good. Tomorrow you can help me vacuum."

She helped me get up from the floor. Imagine Mrs. Oliver being Mary.

SATURDAY,
FEBRUARY 25TH

The worst part of the day was bath time. I'm not a person to expose herself. Yet, I was in a stranger's bathtub being washed. I look at my body; it's hard to remember when my breasts became as long and flat as they are now. I never had much to begin with and used to stuff my padded bras, but now God alone knows. Mrs. Oliver gave me the rag to wash my bottom and vagina. Thank God. She helped me to stand up and dried me as I held on to a towel rack. I was so afraid to let go I couldn't take the end of the towel to dry my private parts.

I kept my bathroom a lot cleaner than Mrs. Oliver keeps hers. I can't stand a dirty bathroom or kitchen. All she has to do is mix a little Clorox with water to get rid of mildew between the tiles. There were several pieces of caked soap in the soap dish. I thought she was going to use them in my rag, but she used a bar of Ivory soap she took from her medicine cabinet.

There's no need worrying over what I can't help, but to think I should come to this. Auntie, my mother, took care of herself until she was nearly 100. My people live long. I'm 75 and can't bathe myself. Come to think of it, Auntie didn't have to worry about falling down in a bathtub. She sat in a big tin basin and bathed outdoors by the side of her house. That's where they found her one lunch time, dead, sitting in her basin.

Mrs. Oliver says that she cared for her mother, nursed her until she died from cancer at 80. She told me this while putting me to bed, such a horrible story. I didn't want to hear about cancer and dying.

I wasn't pleased when Mrs. Oliver woke me up. I thought I hadn't slept, but she said I slept soundly all night.

The bed was wet. My Lord. It must be this strange place. I don't recall wetting myself when I was in my own apartment. Mrs. Taylor, the woman who used to take care of me, woke me up during the night and took me to the bathroom. Diane must have forgotten to tell Mrs. Oliver. Mrs. Oliver changed the bed linen and bathed me. She seemed unconcerned about my wetting the bed. Maybe her mother did the same thing. Well, I'm not her mother, so what she did doesn't soothe my humiliation.

Mrs. Oliver's fifteen-year-old grandson stopped by. He is a big boy who looks like a man. Her daughter came over also, and I could hear them talking in the kitchen.

"Mrs. Nelson came in yesterday. She's a nice old woman," Mrs. Oliver said.

I am an old woman, true, but it's depressing hearing myself being called old.

"When will the other two women come?" her daughter asked.

"Mrs. Price will be here tomorrow. I'm not sure when Miss Turner will come."

I liked listening to them even though they spoke fast, with Southern accents. I could barely understand what they were saying. Last night Mrs. Oliver said she had trouble understanding me: I speak funny. Her daughter is twice her size. Some young people allow themselves to get so out of shape. She couldn't be more than thirty-five. Mrs. Oliver looks as youthful as her girl. They seem to have a good relationship.

I am close to my children. They could talk to me about anything. The older ones still do. I used to get upset when my sister Pearl visited. She undressed in front of them, something I wouldn't do; I didn't think it was right. I was modest even with John. He got a kick out of trying to catch me off guard, undressed, half-dressed—then he would try to pull my clothes off completely. Shy or not, I liked playing with him. Pearl kept the girls up all hours listening to her foolishness about when she was young and telling them her personal business with Desmond, her boyfriend. At her age. I would hear my three younger daughters, Diane, Thelma and Karen, choking with laughter at her stories, and they told her about their lives, things they never told me.

Pearl was more like Auntie than I was—neither of them could resist a compliment from a man. Auntie had the three of us by three different men, and Pearl never married but had two nice boys. Pearl knew her father. I never knew mine and hoped never to know him.

I could never discuss personal things with my children. Children have their place and so do parents. Auntie used to say, "Don't worry about how I live, tend to your own life. I have my place in this world and so do you." I am much closer to my children than Auntie was to us. And I made sure they never experienced the hard work that I did as a little girl. Thank God. I'm proud of my children. But now and again I feel like Auntie must have felt, like a mother whose children think she hadn't done the best for them.

Mrs. Oliver spoke to her husband on the phone. He is in Mississippi, visiting his brother. She said sharply, "Well, what am I to do from here? Just get back any way you can." She slammed the phone down. John and I never spoke to each other like that. I sat with my hand on my chin, my eyes closed. Mrs. Oliver probably thought I was asleep.

Diane called in the afternoon. Mrs. Oliver told her I was fine and seemed happy. I spoke to Diane with Mrs. Oliver standing beside me, so I couldn't tell her about the greens with pork or the cabbage she had given me for lunch. Cabbage gives me gas. I belched a lot and startled Mrs. Oliver when she heard me.

"No one I know burps like that," she said, standing in front of me with her head to one side and her hands on her hips.

Henry used to tell me my belches sounded like something had exploded in me. He said I had enough gas to keep a small nation supplied.

SUNDAY,
FEBRUARY 26TH

I walked around the house a lot today, got tired of
sitting. I went to the kitchen in the back of the house while Mrs.
Oliver was in the bathroom. I have never seen a kitchen with as
many things, two stoves and two refrigerators. I didn't want to
open them. I dislike prying into people's things. Cans and cans of
sodas and beer lined one wall. On a table near one of the refrig-
erators were a bread box, a toaster, an electric grill, a blender and
a mixer. There were mops and three brooms in a corner near the
water cooler. As I walked out of the kitchen I saw another room
and went in. A pile of dirty clothes was heaped in the middle of
the room. It looked like Mrs. Oliver hadn't washed clothes in
months. I had six children, and I washed at least once a week. I
got my feet tangled in a shirt and I almost fell. I managed to
catch hold of the edge of a dresser and felt someone hold me firm.
Mrs. Oliver told me to be careful and to stay out of the room
until she got the washer fixed and the clothes washed. That was
after she agreed she had no excuse for allowing her wash to pile
up. You're right—come let me help you, she said. I told her I
could manage and thanked her. She let me go, and I stood up as
straight as I could and walked out. She followed me out of the
room. I could feel her watching me.

Diane came to the house at one o'clock. She took
me to a Chinese restaurant and ordered chow mein. I don't like
crisp vegetables, and there were plenty on my plate. I ate only a
little; I much preferred Mrs. Oliver's food. I tried to stand up
because I had to use the bathroom, but Diane said, "Please
mother, we aren't finished eating." After only two days, Mrs.
Oliver knew when I had to go. Finally, Diane asked if I had to

use the restroom. When I told her I had asked her to take me ten minutes before, she said I hadn't. I could have sworn I had.

Diane took my hand, and we walked slowly down a long hallway to the restroom. When we got to the door, I felt urine running down my legs. Diane helped me sit on the toilet.

"Mother, I'm sorry. I should have thought..."

But why should she have? How many times have I wet myself in public? Diane wiped my stockings with paper towels. She seemed embarrassed for me, but I was beginning not to care. After all, they say I'm forgetful. I will not get better, but worse.

When we got back to the house, Mrs. Oliver changed my soiled clothing. I just can't get comfortable having this woman whom I hardly know dress and undress me, bathe me, wipe my bottom—such a thing happening to me. What happened that I should come to this?

Sandra called me from New York, but I couldn't talk to her. The vegetables I had eaten at lunch were weighing me down. I could hardly think. Mrs. Oliver told Sandra I was tired and that she should call back tomorrow.

While Mrs. Oliver dressed me for bed, she asked about Sandra. She is an inquisitive woman. I told her Sandra is the eldest of my daughters and that she had been a pretty and bright girl.

MONDAY,
FEBRUARY 27TH

I haven't thought about Sandra much since I've been here. We had such big dreams for her, sent her to the best schools in Jamaica. Then she got married, had three children and settled down. I thought she would do something important with her life. But who am I to say what's important? I never had any education to speak of. After Sandra finished junior college, she got a job as an accountant trainee. She gave us money from her salary. She would buy me fancy negligees that I gave back to her piece by piece at Christmas and on her birthdays, so she could look good for her husband. Lots of young women forget or don't know how to keep a man interested.

I like her husband a lot. I couldn't ask for a better son-in-law, but she gave up her life, stopped working after she married. If I had the opportunities she had, my life would not be what it is. I would have been able to help John more, put away some money and not have to move from place to place. The little money I made from selling our house is practically gone, eaten up from paying Mrs. Taylor to take care of me and rent for an apartment.

My head was killing me tonight. If I had a little rum, I would ask Mrs. Oliver to put some on a piece of cloth and tie it around my head. I noticed some gin and vodka in a cabinet in her living room, but I don't think they would work. She gave me a glass of warm milk and said it would calm me.

I saw John tonight. I felt a pressure on the bed close to me. I thought Mrs. Oliver had come in, but when I opened my eyes, John was sitting on the bed. I couldn't see his face. He sat with his back towards the light from the hallway. I could make out the shape of his head, his ears and the slope of his shoulders. I closed my eyes. If I couldn't see his face, maybe he couldn't see mine. This was the third time I have seen him since I've been here. I see him even more in my dreams. He is usually young, and we are in Jamaica. I think John is waiting for me to join him; maybe he comes to me because he is lonely. I sometimes wonder if John was ready to die or if it mattered to him when his time came. Well, I am not ready to go; I still have things to do and feelings I haven't shared. John will just have to wait. I sat up in bed and he was gone. I turned on the light and took out my diary.

Mrs. Oliver had to help me sit up this morning. I felt so weak; the milk didn't help me sleep, not after I saw John. I spent the rest of the night thinking about my house in Queens. The children tell me not to bother myself about the place, but John and I worked hard to buy it. We didn't want to put money in other people's pockets renting, and we wanted to leave the children something. Those people who bought my house, the Richards, have three boys, and the children have managed in four years to nearly tear the house down. I asked Henry to drive me by the old place before I left New York. Mrs. Richards was in the front yard and asked us to come in. I couldn't believe my eyes when I went inside. The lights on the artificial fireplace were broken; the boys played marbles in the fireplace. Never would my children have destroyed a house the way these people have allowed their children to ruin ours. The walls in Karen's room were marked with crayon drawings. The cornice in the living room, the one I spent good money to have put up, was broken. Children will be children, but if they are properly trained, they will respect things.

At least my bed was dry. I'm not that bad after all.

My headache went away after breakfast. I had grits, eggs and orange juice. I probably shouldn't eat eggs, but they can't make much difference at this point; besides, I like them scrambled, so I ate everything on my plate.

Mrs. Oliver said, "Good, you enjoyed your breakfast, ah?"

Sometimes she speaks to me as if I were a child. I did enjoy her breakfast. If she knows I like it, maybe she will give me the same thing tomorrow.

Diane called, and Mrs. Oliver handed me the phone.

"It's Diane. Speak to her. Tell her what you had for breakfast."

I told Diane I had eaten grits, collard greens with pork and scrambled eggs. Mrs. Oliver took the phone.

"Don't worry. Your mother only had scrambled eggs and grits. I know dear. I'll give her as little fat as possible."

I fell asleep again in the recliner. When I woke up, my legs were crossed. They were so stiff and painful I was afraid my bones would snap like crisp fresh celery if I moved. Mrs. Oliver came to take me to the bathroom, and I couldn't stand up. She uncrossed my legs and rubbed my knees. When I was finally able to get up, I had soiled myself. Lord Jesus. What is happening to me? Diane took me for a complete physical exam before I came to Houston. The doctor didn't say anything about a bladder problem.

A woman was sitting at the dining table when Mrs. Oliver helped me into lunch. Mrs. Oliver introduced her as Mrs. Price. She said she would be sharing my room. Mrs. Price smiled and said hello in a deep low voice. She had light brown hair and a short black beard. She would look better without the beard. Her uneven teeth had food between them. If I still had my own teeth, I would take care of them. I hoped I wouldn't have to share my glass or cup with her. John used to say I was too scornful. "Scawnful dawg nyam dutty pudden." But I get nauseated easily, ever since I was a child. Pearl and I had to share a cup. Most times I cupped my hand and drank out of it, rather than share. Pearl always smelled of the coffee she ground for Auntie every day.

After lunch, Mrs. Oliver helped me into bed and told me to try to take a nap. Mrs. Price sat on the edge of her bed next to mine. Mrs. Oliver half closed the door and left us alone. She could have told me I would be sharing a room with Mrs. Price. It's not easy falling asleep with a person I don't know. I could complain, but what would that change? Where am I to go? I can't stay with Diane; she doesn't even have a place of her own, and Henry isn't expecting me for another year.

Mrs. Price stretched her hands in front of her looking at the lines in her palm. Her beard seemed to have gotten longer. She reminded me of a billy goat I had in Jamaica.

"You probably have a long life line. You don't look even sixty. What are you doing here?" I asked.

"I'm fifty-five. The doctor said I should talk about it as much as possible," she said.

"Fifty-five! You didn't take care of yourself—talk about what?" I asked. I felt sorry for myself but this young woman has a lot of living to do yet.

"Why I'm here. I can't manage on my own. That's what the caseworker told my girl, Clara." Mrs. Price scratched her arm, her neck, and tried to put her hand down the back of her blouse.

"What's the matter with you?"

"My baby girl ran away with my husband."

"Her father? I never..."

"Not her father, my husband. We'll be married three years, soon," she said.

"That's enough to drive a saint mad! What is the world coming to? My God."

"I understand," Mrs. Price said. "They are almost the same age."

"What about common decency? Your own daughter, your husband. I once heard about a woman whose husband took advantage of her daughter. The woman shot him."

Sometimes I wondered if John had another woman. Only God knows what he did when he left me and the children for four years to do farm work. But he always sent money and came home when he could. I tried not to worry about what I didn't know.

"I have to learn to deal with the situation," Mrs. Price said, interrupting my thoughts. She looked at me, holding out her hands.

"Sometimes it's better to be alone. Some men are devils," I told her.

"I don't want to see them, but they wrote me. Dr. Mestel says I should read the letter," she said.

Mrs. Oliver came in and asked why we weren't asleep. I could never force myself to sleep when I wasn't tired.

"When I'm sleepy, I'll sleep," I told her.

"Okay, Mrs. Saucy," she said, and left.

Mrs. Price got under her covers, pulled them up to her nose and closed her eyes. She really is a good-looking woman. Too bad she allowed a man to make her sick. She is still young. If she can't hold one man, she can find another.

TUESDAY, FEBRUARY 28TH

*I hadn't done any dusting in a while, and this morning
I felt in the mood. I waited for Mrs. Oliver to come in so I could ask
for a duster, but I got tired of waiting. I used one of my old undershirts.
Mrs. Price was still sleeping. I worked quietly so I wouldn't disturb her.
I dusted her dresser and mine, my bed and a small table with a plant
on it. I hadn't noticed the plant before. I must ask Mrs. Oliver to put
it in the living room at night; green plants use up oxygen, and I'm
dried up enough as it is.*

*I was amazed at how much dust collected in just a few days.
Even the window sills were filthy. Mrs. Price woke up. She called
out for her husband Milton, asking where he had been.*

*I sat on my bed facing her. She turned over on her back, opened
her eyes and rolled them around in her head. Her eyes were big and
bulgy to begin with, but they looked twice as large. I asked her if I
could help, if she wanted me to call Mrs. Oliver. She called for Milton
again. I told her he wasn't there and to steady herself before her eyes
got stuck in her head.*

*She sat up and covered her face with her hands. Her night-
gown slid off her shoulders exposing her big solid breasts. I can't
think when mine were that firm. I lowered my eyes.*

*I asked her if Milton was the husband who left with her
daughter. She said he was. "Dawg wid too much owna sleep widout
bone," I told her, but I could tell she didn't understand a word I
said. She wanted me to see a letter from Milton and Cathy she had
in her suitcase in the closet. I don't like getting into people's business,
but I didn't want to be impolite.*

*She opened the suitcase, but it was empty. Her hands shook,
and she walked around the room asking for her things. I tried to*

get up, but my knee had gotten stiff. She opened the drawers in the bureau and found her clothes.

She told me to come and see her letter. When I couldn't get up, she pulled me up so suddenly, I thought I heard my knees lock.

She took her clothes out of the drawers, dropping some on the floor. I saw a lovely camisole with fine lace work I haven't seen in years. When we were first married, John's mother gave me a slip with the same beautiful lace on the bodice. Mrs. Price handed me another camisole, panties; my hands were full. Mrs. Oliver walked in, her hands akimbo on her hips, her head leaned to one side and asked what the two of us were doing.

She said this mess wouldn't do, that she was a busy woman, and she started picking the clothes off the floor.

Mrs. Price asked Mrs. Oliver for her letter, but Mrs. Oliver didn't answer; she took the clothes out of my hands and moved me back to my bed. She told Mrs. Price to get back into her bed and to stay in bed until she had her bath ready. She said it was only seven o'clock and we should rest ourselves.

I put my head down on my pillow.

In the afternoon Mrs. Oliver said she had to go to Walgreens and she was taking us with her. She dressed me in the blue suit and white blouse Henry sent me on my last birthday. Mrs. Price dressed herself and Mrs. Oliver combed her hair. The moment I stepped outside I got a chill even though it was a sunny day. I wished I'd had a hat or scarf on. I don't go out in cool weather without covering my ears, head and throat, my weak spots.

Mrs. Price sat in the back seat of the station wagon, and I sat in front with Mrs. Oliver. She didn't bother putting the seat belt around me. I took a tissue from a box on the dashboard, tore off two small pieces and put them in my ears. Mrs. Oliver said, "Now what you want with tissues? You don't have a cold." I just smiled. If I listen to her, I'm likely to get a cold.

We got to Walgreens, and Mrs. Price refused to get out of the car. She looked frightened. Mrs. Oliver told her we didn't have all day, but Mrs. Price moved further back into the seat.

Mrs. Oliver mumbled something under her breath. She rolled down the car window on the front passenger door and locked the doors. She told Mrs. Price to stay in the car and turned to me. She saw the tissue in my ears. Why? she asked, removing my tissues.

The cool air rushed into my ears. What a trial. I knew I would get an earache.

Mrs. Oliver and I walked slowly down each aisle, pushing a shopping cart together. It felt good to be out. A little boy said, "Hi Granny" to me. I smiled at him though I don't like being called granny. I don't mind grandma or Mrs. Nelson. Mrs. Oliver loves to shop. She bought almost everything that was on sale.

I was grateful the cashier rang up the items quickly; I was getting tired and needed to sit down.

When we got back to the car, Mrs. Price was sitting as we left her, and Mrs. Oliver smiled and asked if she was all right. Then she asked me if I had a good outing. I said, Yes, mam. Mam—that's what I hear Mrs. Oliver say. Her grandson also answers her mam. I like that. It shows people still respect each other.

Before Mrs. Oliver put us to bed, she gave us our tranquilizers. She said she hadn't been giving them to us because it hadn't been necessary until this morning's episode. One little incident and she talked as if we had committed a crime. Her day will come.

After she put us to bed, I heard a knock and then I heard another voice. Mrs. Oliver spoke about Mrs. Price. She said someone should tell Mrs. Price she's not going to find that letter. She said Mrs. Price's older daughter, Clara, and the psychiatrist had read the letter.

It's not right. They should tell her those two plan to come see her, Mrs. Oliver said. She said that Mrs. Price will get worse if she sees her daughter and her husband, and I agree with her. What on earth are people coming to? The poor defenseless woman shouldn't have to contend with such nonsense.

I could barely open my eyes this morning, probably because of the tranquilizer. I haven't felt so weak in ages.

Diane called early to tell Mrs. Oliver my doctor asked her to bring me in this morning instead of the following Wednesday. Mrs. Oliver said she would have me ready by ten.

Of all the days the doctor wanted to see me it had to be today when I would be better off in bed sleeping off the weakness. The body has a way of healing itself.

Mrs. Oliver dressed me in the same blouse and suit that I wore yesterday. She probably wanted Diane to see how sharp I looked. What other reason would she have for putting me back into a soiled blouse.

Diane came at ten, and Mrs. Oliver helped her walk me to the car. Diane was concerned. She asked Mrs. Oliver several times what was wrong with me. Mrs. Oliver told her I woke up tired even though I was fine last night.

Diane strapped on the seat belt and put a tape in her cassette player. Some fellow whom I used to know quite well started singing "Memories" in a nice soft voice.

Diane asked me if I liked staying with Mrs. Oliver, if Mrs. Price and I got along, was Mrs. Oliver feeding me well.

"Her daughter ran away with her husband," I answered.

"Whose daughter?"

"Mrs. Oliver says..."

"Mrs. Oliver. Mother, Mrs. Oliver's daughter is married."

"I never said she wasn't."

"Then why would she run away with her father if she is married?"

"I never said she wasn't married, and I never said it was her father. Her mother married this husband three years ago."

"I didn't know Mrs. Oliver recently married."

"Who's talking about Mrs. Oliver?" I said.

"Mother, whom are you talking about?"

"Mrs. Price, you asked me about her didn't you?"

"Did her daughter really run away with her husband?"

My head was beginning to feel too heavy to stay erect. Diane could really wear out a person.

"Mother are you sleeping well?"

I didn't answer her. I needed to be still for a minute.

We got to the office building and Diane went for a wheelchair because I couldn't make the walk from the parking lot to the elevator. Cars coming into the parking garage came dangerously close to us as Diane strained to keep the chair from rolling down a steep incline.

She kept saying, "My God, Mother, I can't seem to hold the chair back."

I pictured myself falling from the chair, down the incline and lying in front of the elevator. I gripped the sides of the chair with what little strength I had. Fortunately, a parking attendant, a good-looking young man, came running up to us and took the handles of the chair from Diane. Diane ran ahead to push the button for the elevator, and I saw him watching her. I don't blame him; she has a sweet figure, like I used to have.

When the doctor took my pressure, it was 130/80.

"What's happening here?" he asked Diane, not looking at me. "Her pressure has gone up."

Diane explained about the elevator and the wheelchair. She told the doctor I had been weak all morning.

The doctor ordered blood and urine tests. Afterwards he told Diane I was dehydrated and had to have a quart of water and four cans of food supplement daily. If I wasn't better by next week, he might put me in the hospital.

"She'll be better," Diane said.

She is such an optimistic girl.

The nice attendant helped Diane wheel me up the incline. She thanked him with a big smile.

When we got back to Mrs. Oliver's, she had already gotten word from the social worker at the doctor's office about the water and supplements. I don't know how I'm to eat and drink the amount of fluids the doctor prescribed.

Diane went back to work, and Mrs. Oliver began enforcing the doctor's orders. She handed me a large glass of water before lunch and one after. By the end of the day, I felt a little sick. I was uncomfortable every time I moved. All together I had four cans of Ensure, the food supplement, and a quart of water.

This is a leap year. People say all sorts of things happen in leap years. They have never brought anything good into my life. John died in a leap year. I don't want to end up in the hospital. I might never come out.

THURSDAY,
MARCH 1ST

Mrs. Oliver came to our room this morning with a little smile on her face.

Today is the first of March, ladies, she said, and then she carried on about the tomatoes she had planted on Monday and had to cover from the frost last night. I told her planting too early and not fertilizing weren't good for vegetables. She asked me what I knew about gardening. Well, I used to have the biggest and juiciest tomatoes on my street in Springfield Gardens, and my squash, big, tasty. Eggshells and vegetable peels to fertilize is the secret, I told her.

I was soaking wet when she removed the covers.

If you keep this up, you'll have to sleep in a life jacket, she said.

The things I have to put up with. I got a chill when she put me in a tub of lukewarm water. She took me out, wrapped a blanket around me and sat me in front of a gas heater. She should have realized that after I had lain in my urine all night, a hot bath would have been better. She turned the heater on high; the flames leapt from behind the iron grid. She gave me a chill and then tried to catch me on fire. I tried to push the chair back, away from the flames, but couldn't budge it. I called out to her and told her I was about to be burned up. She called me a coward then turned down the heater.

Mrs. Price came in the bedroom and sat with me. Again she started on the letter, asking me if she had told me about it. I didn't want to hear or talk about anything, but what could I do. I told her I knew about the letter and her husband. I didn't mention what I heard Mrs. Oliver say last night about her daughter and husband visiting.

She pulled the blanket closer around my neck and legs and asked me if I was still cold. Pray the day never comes when you start wetting yourself like me, I said to her. She asked me my age, and then told me she hoped to live as long as I did.

She told me her husband Milton was 25. I don't believe I would ever have married a man 30 years younger than I. I remember how vexed I was with John when I found out he had lied about his age; he said he was two years older than he was. By the time he told me the truth, he had my heart—I had agreed to marry him.

Mrs. Price said she had an appointment to see her psychiatrist tomorrow. She is supposed to tell him she read the letter, but she can't find it. She wanted me to tell her what to say to the doctor. Tell him you can't find it. Ask him if he read it. It won't hurt to ask, I told her. She hung her head and said she couldn't do that.

Mrs. Oliver said she had a hard day, so we all went to bed early. She gave Mrs. Price a tranquilizer which didn't help because she talked and laughed in her sleep. At least she was happy. I'm sleeping in the same room with a woman who is almost out of her mind. What if she should take me for Milton or her daughter and strangle me in my sleep, or worse yet, stab me? I never imagined dying violently. Well, I hope God will keep Mrs. Price's head clear.

FRIDAY,
MARCH 2ND

Mrs. Oliver sang and hummed to herself while I ate my breakfast alone. Mrs. Price was dressed and sat in the living room waiting for her daughter to take her to the doctor. She looked nice. Mrs. Oliver had brushed her hair to the side, curled and then pinned the ends with a large barrette. I didn't notice her beard so much. Mrs. Oliver might have brushed it under her chin. She folded her shaking hands in her lap.

What a day! I'm glad I'm an old woman. I have put up with all the nonsense young people are just beginning to experience. Not that I wouldn't mind being young again. I was a contented woman in my twenties and thirties, and even before John died. The worst period in my life was when I first got married. John's mother thought their family better than mine, and she was probably right, if I'm to give credit where it's deserved. But who was she to point up my family's shortcomings to me and hold me responsible. I'm only one woman and as she saw later on, I lived the best way I knew how and raised my children to be decent people. I don't hold a grudge against her because she came around to seeing things my way.

My feet were a little swollen, so after breakfast Mrs. Oliver put me in the recliner and pushed me way back to elevate my feet. I hoped Diane wouldn't visit today. If she saw my feet, she would take me to the doctor.

I don't recall the exact time, but it must have been close to lunch because Mrs. Oliver was watching Days of Our Lives. *If I carried on like the people in the soap operas, I would have died early. Most of them have no decency. They don't care about anything but sex. But too much of one thing can get very boring. Someone knocked on the door. Mrs. Oliver turned the TV down.*

She got up to answer the door. A young man and woman came in and asked for Mrs. Price. Mrs. Oliver told them she went to the doctor. The young woman said she was Mrs. Price's daughter and asked if they could wait. Mrs. Oliver told them to sit down and said in a hard voice, "You can wait, but I don't know how long she'll be."

I sat up in my chair. I wished they would leave the poor sick woman alone. Some people want everything. They will bleed you to death if you don't keep your eyes open. The girl took her mother's husband! What did they want now—her blessings? The old-time saying is true, "Pawsen cirssen im pickney fuss." I sat back in the chair, put my hand on my head and looked at them. They sat on the couch close to each other. She was a real pretty little girl. She had her mother's brown complexion and light brown hair. I couldn't make out her eyes or his since they were sitting across the room. I can tell what people are like from their eyes. He was skinny and didn't look as young as twenty-five. He had Jerri curls all over his head. I don't mind them so much on women, but I don't like them on men. I couldn't imagine what Mrs. Price saw in him. He definitely would never be my cup of tea. I like more body to go with the man. If I can hardly see him with his clothes on, what will he look like when he takes them off? It didn't look as if he had anything in his pants' front. Not that size is all that counts, but a man should have a little something to make a woman feel good. The children would be surprised if they read this. I must say it is only as I have gotten older that I have the courage to talk about sex. As an old woman I worry less about what people think and what I thought I had to believe.

A car door slammed, and Milton and Cathy jumped. The older daughter, Clara, came in ahead of Mrs. Price. When she saw her sister and Milton, she moved in front of her mother, but Mrs. Price saw them. Clara and Mrs. Oliver went behind Mrs. Price as she reached out and said, Milton, Cathy...Then she started screaming. I remember once walking past a slaughter house and hearing a cow bawl out after that first cut. The pain in the cow's wail made

me shiver as it did today when Mrs. Price cried out. She flung herself
on the floor. They all bent over her. Her daughter Cathy cried, told
her mother that she loved her. She begged Mrs. Price to stop. Well
said, but too late, I would say. Everything was happening at once.
A neighbor came over and held Mrs. Price. Mrs. Oliver called an
ambulance and the police. Somebody put me in the bedroom and
closed the door, but I opened it and watched them take Mrs. Price
away. Clara began shouting at Cathy and Milton, "Get out you
bastards. Look at Ma, look at Ma."
   Some day! It's so quiet here now without Mrs. Price.

   I have been with Mrs. Oliver a little over a week,
though it seems longer. Mrs. Oliver says that on Monday
another woman, over ninety, will be coming to stay with us. If
she has any children, they are probably close to my age. Things
should slow down a bit with her here. She is too old a hen to
have any young roosters sporting after her.
   Diane called and told me she would take me to an
Ethiopian restaurant on Sunday. When I asked her what kind of
food they cooked, she said the food was hot and spicy. I told her
I didn't want to have to begin taking pressure pills again, but
she said they would prepare the food whichever way I liked it.
I'm looking forward to going. Diane loves to eat out. I keep
telling her to learn how to cook and save money; however, it's
nice going out once in a while—no need killing herself over a
stove.
   A repairman finally came and fixed Mrs. Oliver's washing
machine. I hadn't been in that back room since the first time I
almost broke my neck, but I'm sure there are a lot more dirty
clothes. I'm down to just a few underwear and gowns.
   I told Mrs. Oliver I would help her wash. She thanked me
but said she could manage. She let me push the vacuum cleaner,
and I dusted the living room. I have been cleaning house most
of my life. I don't understand why Mrs. Oliver cleaned behind
me. She dusted the same table I dusted twice, and she picked

up things off the carpet I vacuumed. Some people just aren't satisfied; you can never please them. She took an ashtray I had forgotten on the floor and put it on the table. The mind is not all it used to be. They smoke too darn much anyway, she and her daughter.

Tonight Mrs. Oliver asked me what I'm always writing. When I told her I was keeping a diary, she said, "I hope you're not writing about me."

"I write about anything. It's my diary," I told her.

"Okay, missy, whatever you say."

I think I'll find somewhere to keep my diary so she won't read it; I wouldn't put it past her to go into my personal things. It may be ridiculous for an old lady to keep a diary, but I'm going to continue writing.

I've never done so much nothing in my life. On Sundays I would cook a special dinner for John and the children. Then I would relax. I tried to keep the Sabbath even if I didn't go to church as often as I sent the children. Every day is a Sabbath for me. Now the only reason I know it's Sunday is because Diane takes me out to dinner. But it's no good for me to go on this way. I only end up with a headache which is bound to speed up the deterioration of my brain. I have been spending much of my time lately thinking about what is happening to my brain. I have very little else to do, and I scare myself imagining what might eventually happen to me. Soon, I think, I'll begin to smell the sore spot I think of as my brain. Diane thinks I'm depressed. She doesn't want to believe the doctors. If I tried hard enough, I would be just fine, she tells me. I used to think the same thing, that this is something I could get over. But sometimes I wake up with thoughts that aren't mine, and I get so weary I wish I could shut my eyes forever.

A strong gust of wind this morning sounded as if it would take off the side of the house. The glass in the windows shook as if they would fall out. I will never forget that storm in Jamaica in fifty-four or fifty-five. The sky turned red and black. I was worried but excited for it to strike and be finished with. All those weather reports, scaring people. Plenty of us boarded up our houses, but that didn't help a lot of people. John and I boarded the windows, the door and the lattice work. When the winds and rain began tearing through the trees, the little old house started squeaking and water poured in through a hole John had patched. We rolled the four children, my three and my cousin Marie's son, Johnny, between our big mattress then sat down in the darkness talking quietly, listening to branches breaking from the trees. We thanked God the next morning when we saw that the big light pole across from our house had fallen down away from it. If that pole had hit the house, we would have died. God will only take us when he's ready. Three days after the storm, poor Johnny got knocked down by a motorcycle and died on the spot. Imagine, after living through that hell of a storm. When our time comes, it comes.

The sun came up and the sky was blue with small puffy white clouds. It was a perfect morning for gardening. If I were Mrs. Oliver I would have been outside digging and fertilizing my tomatoes. She spends a lot of time working in the house and driving all over the place. She needs to be outdoors more, clear her mind and walk some. I would gladly have walked with her on such a beautiful morning.

Mrs. Oliver came in the room and saw me looking out the window.

"Nice day, ah," she said.

"That's right. You should be outside in your garden. Those tomatoes can't take care of themselves."

"Okay, Mrs. Nelson, I tell you what, after breakfast we'll go out together. I'm not going to church until this evening."

We went out after breakfast. I didn't feel sleepy, like I usually do after eating. Mrs. Oliver brought me a pillow and helped me down on my knees. She has a small garden plot, only tomatoes and peas. Squash and corn would grow well here in the black soft soil. I put some of the dirt to my nose and looked closely at it.

"Don't you go eating any of that now," Mrs. Oliver said.

"You just fed me. What do you think, I've lost all my marbles?"

"Only telling you," she said.

I've seen people eat worse things. The body knows what it needs, and dirt is full of minerals. I felt like putting the handful of dirt in my mouth. Who does she think I am?

I did a terrible thing. I pulled out one of the tomato plants that I thought was a weed. Mrs. Oliver replanted it and said it was time for me to go in. I had a hard time getting up and walking back to the house. My body felt as if it were in plaster of Paris. When I sat down in the recliner, I thought my back would crack open down my spine. Mrs. Oliver gave me a can of strawberry food supplement. Strawberries make me nauseated. I drank it quickly and asked for a peppermint candy. I sat back in the recliner, rolling the mint around in my mouth. I noticed the dirt under my fingernails. I felt good. I used to be such a gardener.

I had slept for about an hour when Clara, Mrs. Price's daughter, came in. She looked good in her purple dress. She sat down on the sofa and asked how I was. I told her that I was still breathing and asked her about her mother. She said that she was fine and would be out of the hospital soon. She asked Mrs. Oliver if she would consider taking her mother back. She had nowhere else to take her. Mrs. Oliver said she was willing to try, but she didn't want Cathy or Mrs. Price's husband coming back in her house. I'm glad Mrs. Price will be coming back.

Diane called. She wasn't feeling well. She had cramps, so she wouldn't make it over until tomorrow during her lunch hour. She could just as well wait until the weekend. I know Diane cares, and I also know that she doesn't enjoy seeing me that much. She thinks it's her duty not to miss a visit. She feels guilty leaving me here, but it's not her fault that I'm old and sick, or that John died, and I'm having a hard time living without him. It's not my fault either. Sandra also called me. I told her I helped Mrs. Oliver in the garden. She sounded surprised, like she didn't believe me.

When I gave the phone back to Mrs. Oliver, she said, "She sure was out in the garden, did a real good job too. Your mother must have had a nice garden."

She will say anything, Mrs. Oliver.

My scalp has been itching me all night. I must tell Mrs. Oliver that my hair needs washing and oiling.

MONDAY,
MARCH 5TH

Miss Turner came today. She doesn't have a wrinkle on her face, only a few folds near her lips and under her neck. She is a small nice-looking woman. As bent over as I am, I am still a good foot taller than she. Her hair is completely white and shiny, two plaits wrapped around her head. I could be wrong, but she looks as if she has all her own teeth. I lost my top ones early, the bottom teeth one by one when I was in my forties. I have been very particular about my teeth, but you can't get gold from silver. I had a bad start. Auntie lost her teeth at twenty. I saw to it that my children got plenty of milk and took them to the dentist as often as we could afford. Diane and Sandra have the best teeth, strong. Henry is like me. He already has a partial bridge.

Miss Turner's niece, Dorothy, came with her. I heard them say Dorothy is a lawyer; it's wonderful to see a young black woman with so much education. She carried herself well and looked very professional in her gray tailored dress. She was like a giant next to her aunt. They don't resemble each other in any way. Dorothy is big-boned; she has a broad mouth and small eyes. Mrs. Turner has a face like a bird, pointed nose, mouth and head.

Dorothy didn't stay long because she had an appointment, but she told her aunt she would be back tomorrow. Miss Turner didn't answer her niece. Don't tell me there is going to be more trouble here. Miss Turner didn't look happy either. Mrs. Oliver had cleaned out the back room; she put Miss Turner and her suitcases there. I didn't see her for the rest of the day. At supper time, Mrs. Oliver put food on a tray and took it to the room.

I ate alone and thought about Miss Turner. I suppose she would have shared my room with me. Maybe Mrs. Oliver thinks it's better not to get Miss Turner used to my room since Mrs. Price will be back soon.

Mrs. Oliver sneezed most of the evening. I told her to drink some strong tea with a little brandy and lime juice and to go to bed early. She said it was a good idea, but after she put me in bed, I could hear her out in the living room talking on the phone. She agrees very easily to what people say, but never takes advice. Well, no one knows everything. I'll know better than to give suggestions to her in the future. I have taken heed even from children. One can learn from anyone, even an old lady.

Diane didn't go to work today, so she didn't come to see me. She still isn't feeling well. I wish I could take care of her though she said her roommate Robin would help her. Diane is not a girl to complain. Don't worry mother, she said. As if I am supposed to lose all my feelings along with my mind. She is my child, and I'll worry.

TUESDAY,
MARCH 6TH

I'm anxious to see Diane. If she is not better by tomorrow, I'm going to ask Mrs. Oliver to take me to see her.

Thank God my children have been healthy. Thelma is the only one who ever got seriously sick. She was about nine or ten and got a high fever. Auntie sent me some Jack In The Bush that I boiled down and fed to Thelma. When that didn't break the fever, we gave her garlic tea. The next morning the fever was gone, but Thelma had a cricked neck; she couldn't move her head. Mrs. Simpson, God bless her soul, always helping me out, said it looked like Thelma had a stroke from being exposed to the moonlight while sleeping. She went and got Millie Miller, a left-hander who we believed could cure a cricked neck. Millie twisted Thelma's head, and the child looked as if she would be all right, except the next morning she couldn't move her arms or legs. I rubbed her with camphor and eucalyptus oil, but she seemed paralyzed. Millie and a few other neighbors started whispering about obeah. I believe anything is possible, and I had seen some things in my days; however, I didn't want to think anyone would do evil to my children, and to tell the truth I thought Millie was being bad-minded because she couldn't help Thelma. John was away, but if he had been at home, he would have told them where to put their obeah—nothing but foolishness, he claimed. I would tell him not to close his mind, leave himself defenseless. Fortunately, I didn't listen to that obeah talk and took Thelma to Dr. Aikens. He put her in the hospital immediately. She had rheumatic fever. He looked after my child as he would his own. He said her recovery was a miracle because her heart wasn't affected.

Miss Turner was at breakfast when Mrs. Oliver brought me to the table. She looked fresh and clean in a pink long-sleeved blouse and blue skirt.

I said I was glad to see her since I didn't have a chance to speak to her yesterday, welcome her properly. She said she was fine; she hadn't been in the mood for company, nor did she require any welcome since she wouldn't be in Mrs. Oliver's house if she had anything to say about her welfare.

We ate in silence, and Miss Turner went to her bedroom right after breakfast. She walks with a cane but doesn't need any help. The problem with my brain has really affected my body, and so quickly. When I first came to Houston, I weighed almost a hundred pounds; a couple of days ago I was down to eighty-five pounds. Diane asked Mrs. Oliver to watch me because I walk around, but she could have saved her breath. Some days I can barely get up out of the recliner, and when I'm up, it's hard to get my balance because I have to push myself up out of the chair with so much force. If Mrs. Oliver hadn't been in the room with me yesterday, I would have knocked myself out against the wall when I got up. I look at Miss Turner, and I can't help but feel sorry for myself.

Mrs. Oliver fixed barbecued chicken with squash and black-eyed peas for lunch. She loves to cook. My top denture has been pinching my gums for about a week now, so I took them out even though Diane is worried I'm losing weight because I can't eat properly without my teeth. But I can eat without them. My gums are sore, but they hurt more with the teeth in. Diane said she will take me to the dentist on Thursday to get the dentures relined if she is feeling better. I don't think my teeth have anything to do with my weight, but who am I to say.

Miss Turner didn't eat much at lunch. Mrs. Oliver looked mad. She didn't force Miss Turner though, the way she would have threatened to feed me.

"If I were you, I would eat before it gets cold. I'm not warming that food again."

Miss Turner doesn't take anything lying down. Right away she told Mrs. Oliver she was not asking for any favors; hot or cold, food was food.

Mrs. Oliver looked at Miss Turner and then left us to vacuum her bedroom. She must be feeling sorry for Miss Turner or else she would have given her a talking to. When we were alone, I asked Miss Turner if she didn't like living with us. She said she had had no intentions of changing her living situation. Her niece put her here without her consent, most likely encouraged by her husband. She had taken care of herself without a problem until she forgot to turn off the stove and Dorothy came in and smelled gas. Dorothy insisted it wasn't the first time. I sympathized with Miss Turner. I told her the same thing happened to me, worse. My kids said I left pots burning on the stove without water or anything in them. Miss Turner said she and I were two different stories. She is right; she could live another twenty years as strong and sharp as she is. But she is pining over her house, the one she said Dorothy and her husband plan to live in. All that worry will take a toll on her system. At least family will be living in her house. My house was sold to strangers. They have cemented over my garden, put in a basketball court.

You might be better off here, I told her, but she didn't want to hear that. She had worked hard, saved for a comfortable life in her old age only to see her plans come to naught. She would be better off in another world, she said.

Sometimes I feel I have left this world and come back another person. I can't be the same Hortense Nelson who, until ten years ago, had a husband, a home, friends, all my children and grandchildren around me. I asked her if she looked in the mirror much. She just stared at me and said I was being incoherent, rambling from one thing to the next. She and her mother were both teachers and taught until they were well into their seventies, she was proud to tell. I might not be half the person I used to be, and I couldn't speak for my father, but my mother had all her faculties in order until the day she died, I told her.

I asked Mrs. Oliver to call Diane. Diane said she was better and would take me to the dentist on Thursday. I told her about Miss Turner, and she said she was glad I had company again.

Later in the evening, I heard Mrs. Oliver tell Dorothy over the phone that her aunt wasn't eating and that she didn't want any problems, so maybe they should find somewhere else for Miss Turner. Mrs. Oliver saw me watching her.

"You ready for bed?"

"No," I answered.

"Well, I'm ready for mine," she said.

She massaged my knees after she took off my socks. She sometimes does this before I go to bed; it's a little ticklish, but it feels good.

I asked her if she dressed Miss Turner for bed.

"I help her, but she can do it herself. She thinks she can do everything. They should have left her to do for herself or get someone to live in. They just don't want to spend the money."

She told me to keep my feet under the covers and asked if I wanted her to leave my socks on.

"My toes need some fresh air; leave the socks off," I said.

Dorothy stopped by to speak to Miss Turner before breakfast. I waited at the table, hungry. I eat a lot lately, but eating doesn't help. The food seems to evaporate through my pores. Mrs. Oliver was in the living room with Miss Turner and Dorothy, and kept excusing herself to check the biscuits in the oven. Each time she opened the oven a fresh, sweet, buttery smell came out. Dorothy might have been considerate enough to come by after breakfast, or Mrs. Oliver could have invited her to eat with us. Mrs. Oliver always cooks enough for company.

Dorothy wore a navy blue suit and a white silk blouse, with a high collar that made her neck seem longer than I had remembered. She sat close to the window, and I could see her face well—too much rouge. She sat on the edge of the sofa leaning towards her aunt and playing nervously with the handle on her small brown briefcase.

"Aunt Mary, you can't continue this. If you don't want to stay here, then come and live with Sam and me."

"Under no circumstances will I live with that man. You can let his big smile and talk fool you. I didn't help put you through school for you to end up with someone like him. He has no ambition. You have my house. What more do you want?" Miss Turner said, turning away from Dorothy.

"I won't argue with you about Sam. But if you refuse to stay with us, what do you want me to do?"

Dorothy looked ashamed. Miss Turner didn't hold back with her words. I felt sorry for the young woman, but my heart was with Miss Turner. A lot of people let passion rule their hearts. Dorothy continued talking to her aunt, asking her to cooperate with Mrs. Oliver. She begged her to eat until she could work something out.

I interrupted them to ask Mrs. Oliver to check the biscuits.

Miss Turner went to her room, and Mrs. Oliver and Dorothy spoke at the front door. Mrs. Oliver told Dorothy her aunt would come to her senses when she realized that she couldn't take care of herself.

"She'll eat, even if I have to feed her. You go on to work and don't worry about a thing. I'll keep her as long as you want her to stay here," Mrs. Oliver assured her.

Last night she told me Miss Turner could take care of herself; now she says she can't. That woman will say anything.

She placed the food on the table, scrambled eggs, grits, biscuits, bananas and juice. With a stern look, she went to get Miss Turner.

"Your food is on the table," she said to Miss Turner.

"Leave me alone," Miss Turner said.

I didn't hear any voices, then I heard Miss Turner cry out, "Help me, oh God. Leave me alone."

Mrs. Oliver and Miss Turner came out into the dining room. Mrs. Oliver held Miss Turner firmly under one arm and led her to a chair. The old woman hung her head, groaning. I was so upset I couldn't eat. Miss Turner wasn't eating either. At ninety, a woman should be able to have her own way. If they left her alone she would eat. She groaned. Mrs. Oliver looked at me.

"Now Mrs. Nelson, eat—you eat like a horse, so eat."

"How can I eat with all this going on?" I asked her.

She picked up our plates and said, "Breakfast is over."

Miss Turner went in the back, and Mrs. Oliver started her morning cleaning. She was singing as if nothing had happened. I sat in my recliner and wondered what John was thinking, seeing me in this house. I heard Miss Turner moaning from the back room, so I decided to check on her. The room seemed so far. She lay curled up on her side and looked like a little girl until I saw her face. I asked her if I could come in, but she didn't answer. I went in and sat down on a big metal trunk near her bed.

"I don't really want to be here either, but it's my daughter Diane's turn to take care of me. She came to Houston, so I'm here. To tell the God's truth, I would rather be in New York. I had visitors in New York, and all my other children except one live there. But if I live to see next year, I'll be back in New York with my son," I told her. She turned and looked past me as if I were invisible. I asked her if her husband was dead.

"I never married," she said proudly.

"Have any children?" I asked.

"I never married, I said. Dorothy is my only living relative."

"I don't know what I would do without my children."

"Some people depend too much on their children." She sighed deeply and fell asleep with her mouth open. I could tell her teeth were false, good ones. She must have spent a lot on them.

Miss Turner ate ice cream at dinner. Mrs. Oliver didn't have to say a word to me because I was half starved. Miss Turner asked for a second bowl of ice cream. Mrs. Oliver told her she would probably get a stomachache, but she gave her the ice cream anyway. She was glad Miss Turner was finally eating something.

Mrs. Oliver's grandson, Ronnie, came over at about eight o'clock to sit with us while Mrs. Oliver went with her daughter to a chorale recital. He brought a big portable tape player which looked as if it would give him a hernia.

Miss Turner and I had just begun watching *Dynasty* when he came in. He was a polite boy, said good evening to both of us. Ronnie put a tape in his recorder, put in his earphones. After a few minutes, started laughing. He covered his mouth with his hand and didn't answer when Miss Turner asked him what he was listening to.

I waved my hand at him, and he stopped the tape and took off his earphones. Miss Turner asked him again what tape he was listening to.

"Richard Pryor. He's a comedian, mam."

"I know who he is. Let's hear him. Turn the television down, let's hear it."

"I don't think you want to hear this, mam," Ronnie said.

"Yes, I do," Mrs. Turner said, making herself more comfortable in the chair.

He pushed the play button. I have heard rude calypso songs but never so much swearing on one tape. Every other word was f—— or motherf——. Unnecessary, I thought, but a joke was a joke, I guess. Miss Turner squeezed her lips tight and laughed. She made sneezing sounds that got louder and louder. When she couldn't hear something, she had Ronnie rewind the tape and turn up the volume. When that Pryor man told about some monkey that put his thing into people's ears until he got him some monkey pussy, Miss Turner threw her head back and stiffened her short legs straight out in front of her. I laughed a little, mostly inside. Jesus, if my son, Henry, could see his mother. Ronnie got us some more ice cream, and we listened to the other side of the tape.

Ronnie asked us not to tell his grandmother he played that tape for us. I'll never say a word, and I'm certain Miss Turner won't either.

THURSDAY, MARCH 8TH

Mrs. Oliver gave me breakfast, and I was dressed and waiting for Diane. Mrs. Oliver placed my sweater on the arm of the recliner. I told her I needed something to cover my head and ears. She brought me a scarf that looked as old as I am, but it was clean. She tied it around my head, stepped back and smiled.

Don't you look cute, she said.

We got to the dentist's office at ten o'clock, a woman dentist, Dr. Fine, who took care of geriatric patients. Diane had searched to find someone like her. The first time she had tried to take me to a dentist, at one of those family clinics, they took one look at me and said they weren't equipped to handle people like me. Dr. Fine was a patient woman. She has my sympathies. When she tried to put my upper plate in, it hurt so much, I clenched my gums together. She told me she would work as quickly as possible but she needed to get the plate in my mouth. I opened as wide as I could, but my jaws came together on their own. Finally she got the plate in, made an impression and took X-rays. Diane had to hold the small plastic tabs in my mouth. They put a heavy protective apron on her, but one can never tell about X-rays.

Dr. Fine showed Diane the impressions and said my bite was off because my gums had shrunk. She cleaned and relined the plates and left them in my mouth. They felt a lot tighter, uncomfortable. Diane was quite pleased that the plates fit me; if only she knew how much they were hurting. Dr. Fine said I should be able to eat a better variety of foods. I have been having trouble with my food, but Mrs. Oliver crushes my vegetables, and I usually chew all the juices out of my meat she cuts up in small pieces. Diane thinks I will gain some weight now. The doctors in New York told my children I had heart failure and my blood was unable to carry nutrients as it should. I think that is my problem, not my teeth.

We stopped at a Kentucky Fried Chicken place. I guess Diane was anxious to see how my relined dentures worked. I couldn't eat the chicken. Poor Diane got upset. She went into a grocery store nearby and brought back two bottles of baby food: meat and pineapple-banana. I was glad she had the sense to ask me first if I would mind eating bottled foods. The meat was tasteless. The fruit was all right, but it wasn't fun sitting next to Diane, smelling the fried chicken and not being able to eat it.

Diane didn't just seem upset; she looked worried. She will hardly talk about herself. Her friends and sisters bend her ears with their problems even when she has more than her own share, but she doesn't like to admit she is anything but fine. I was like that too. I could speak to John about anything but with no one else.

I told her she seemed upset. She said, I'm fine Mother. I told her that I wasn't born yesterday, and I was worried about her.

She admitted her company had laid off people again— engineers, managers, twenty people last week—and they planned more layoffs next week. Since she has been working there less than a year, she thinks she'll get laid off and have to go back to New York.

I told her to look for another job, but Lord knows I wouldn't mind going back to New York. Besides, that will give Diane and Andrew a chance to get back together. They have been seeing each other for nine years. After two people have spent that many years in a relationship, they should put down roots together. But because he didn't stay with her in Houston when he couldn't find a job, Diane is holding it against him. She could have gone back with him. Time waits for no man. She worries about my aging, my illness, but I told her the older I get, the older she gets.

Would you have gone back if you were me? she asked me.

Maybe not with a man like Andrew, but I would have gone anywhere with John back when the kids were small and I was young. What else would I have done? These are different times. I told her maybe she should date someone else. She smiled and said, Mother, there is no dating without sex these days.

I never mentioned sex. Leave well enough alone then, I said.

When we got back Mrs. Oliver put me down for a nap, and I slept until dinner. I dreamt Diane and Andrew got married. She wore a beautiful white satin gown with hand-tatted lace and a six-foot-long train. She carried a huge bouquet of flowers, so big it covered her face. Her eyes were closed—a bad sign. I was uneasy when I woke up. Whenever I dreamt about weddings, I was sure to hear about a death. Who would it be this time?

Miss Turner was asleep in Mrs. Price's bed when I got up. Mrs. Oliver called to her from the hallway, but she didn't move. Mrs. Oliver came in, saw her in the bed and left her there.

FRIDAY,
MARCH 9TH

I woke up before dawn with dread in my heart. I couldn't let go of the dream about the wedding. It could very well be meant for me. My tongue was sore too. I shouldn't have gone to bed with my dentures in, but Dr. Fine told Diane I should keep them in overnight.

If I didn't think Mrs. Boone, my oldest friend, was already dead, I would have thought my dream was meant for her; but twice when Diane spoke about her, she said Mrs. Boone was a nice lady. I haven't heard a word from her since I've been in Houston. Nobody thinks of calling her for me. I don't remember her telephone number, and I used to speak to her every day. I have thought to ask Diane if she is dead, but I'm not ready to know for sure.

The heaviness in my chest got stronger. I felt as if someone was sitting on me. I took deep breaths but had trouble letting them out. I breathed quickly, feeling the fear move up from my toes to my chest. I have been afraid many times in my life and know eventually everything passes, but I felt as if I were being carried away and at any time that moment would come when I could no longer help myself. I recited the Twenty-Third Psalm. I can't tell how many times I said, For thou art with me. When I said, Yea, though I walk through the valley of the shadow of death, my head felt like it was melting. I repeated, For thou art with me, until I fell asleep.

I woke up several times, feeling weak all over. Once I closed my eyes and saw myself in a coffin, a plain wood box. My eyes were closed, but I could see that I was struggling to open them. In my dream, I wore red lipstick, a thing I rarely used. I raised my hand and wiped my mouth. The thought of having people see me lying in a box, looking so bony, to have them scared of seeing me, of having the children afraid of me, I don't like at all.

Miss Turner stood in front of me wearing a short-sleeved blue and white polka dot dress with a black shawl thrown over her shoulders. She leaned over me, smiling with one finger pressed against her lips then turned and floated out of the room.

I took out my dentures. The sun came up, and the bad feeling in my chest was gone, but my tongue was still sore.

Mrs. Oliver came in and found the teeth on the bed and tried to force them back in my mouth. I couldn't help crying out. She asked if they hurt and when I said yes, she shook her head and walked out of the room with them. She came back with them in a glass of water which she put on the dresser. She went to Miss Turner's bed and pulled back the covers, but Miss Turner was gone. Mrs. Oliver rushed out of the room. I heard her go into the bathroom, the hallway, calling out Miss Turner's name. She came and asked me if I had seen Miss Turner. I told her how I had seen her in my dream.

Mrs. Oliver called Dorothy, then went outside to look for Miss Turner. She passed by my bedroom window twice. She hadn't combed her hair and looked like a wild woman. I had a feeling Miss Turner was fine.

Mrs. Oliver came in and put my robe on me and helped me into the living room. I don't like sitting undressed, my mouth smelling like my feet, and my hair uncombed. I'm used to being bathed and fed first. I know Mrs. Oliver was upset, but she could have left me in the bedroom.

I sat in the living room for a short time when a man yelled through the front screen door for Mrs. Oliver. He startled me. Mrs. Oliver might not mind running around unwashed, but I do. I told him I would call Mrs. Oliver for him so he wouldn't have to come in, but before I could get up, he walked in with Miss Turner. She leaned heavily on her cane. He lives in the neighborhood and saw Miss Turner sitting at the bus stop on his way back from taking his wife to work. Mrs. Oliver thanked him and offered him a cup of coffee. He said no and left in a hurry.

"Your niece is on her way. I'll let her deal with you," Mrs. Oliver said.

Miss Turner smiled. I have to hand it to her, she never gives up. Her face looked bright and healthy. There's nothing like a walk to get the blood flowing.

When Dorothy came, she went straight to her aunt and insisted on an explanation. Miss Turner said she had wanted to see a lawyer to straighten out her business.

Dorothy reminded her aunt that she took care of her business. She called her aunt a willful, childish and selfish person who didn't care if she made people worry. Miss Turner told her niece that she was seeking advice about what Dorothy was doing to her. That's when Dorothy got angry. She gave Miss Turner three choices: either stay with Mrs. Oliver and act civilly, pack right away and go home with Dorothy or think about a nursing home. Miss Turner looked helpless.

She groaned all night. It was worse than listening to someone snore.

Miss Turner was sitting up in bed brushing her hair when I opened my eyes. I had a restless night listening to her moans.

"Don't tell me you're going out again?" I asked her.

"No, no. A fortune teller lived next door to me. She asked me several times to read my fortune, and I refused. I heard she was accurate too. If I could have foreseen all this..." she said.

"I wouldn't want to know beforehand," I told her. "If I had been able to see how much of my life I would waste, I wouldn't have lasted this long. It's much easier to let time gradually slip by, so each day I can say, I'll do better tomorrow."

"I should have sold my house a long time ago and moved into an apartment. I have a couple of friends who have moved to Florida and are happy. Gertrude Howard moved there after her husband died. She lives with another woman. I'm going to write her today," she said, sighing.

When she mentioned Florida, I remembered a tune John learned while he did farm work there. Not for my life could I think of the words. I hummed the tune and asked Miss Turner if she knew the name of the song, but she had never heard of it. It's possible I had the tune wrong, but it was strong in my mind. I could see John's mouth while he was singing it, his lips frilled on one side so that I could see the metal clasp on his dentures. He loved that song. I tried to remember it all day long. I must ask Diane about it.

Miss Turner asked Mrs. Oliver for paper and pen. Mrs. Oliver gave her a few sheets of notebook paper, and Miss Turner asked if she didn't have any decent writing paper in the house. Miss Turner has a steady neat handwriting. I sat beside her as she wrote, murmuring to herself. After she wrote three pages, she asked for an envelope. Mrs. Oliver didn't have any stamps but promised to take the letter to the post office.

Later, Mrs. Oliver's husband called.

"It's over four weeks; are you married to your brother? I'm not sending anything. I work hard. You and your family better not look to me for a dime. If you're out of cash come home." Then she said in a low voice, "See you."

How a man can stay away from a woman who can cook like Mrs. Oliver is beyond me.

Mrs. Oliver found a pressure sore on the lower part of my back during my bath. I had one before when Mrs. Taylor took care of me. The doctor told Diane the sore could be dangerous and to bring me in if it didn't begin to heal soon. My back had been itchy for a while but I didn't feel a sore. Mrs. Oliver left me in the tub. She came back carrying a small tin container. She dried me and put whatever was in the can on the sore. It stung, and I tried to rub it off, but she held my hand and said it would burn just a little while. I asked her what it was, and she told me I didn't have to know everything. It's my back, I should know.

Whatever it was smelled horrible, so I didn't press her. She sat on my bed and brushed my hair; it felt good. She had never brushed my hair before. She must really miss her husband.

SUNDAY, MARCH 11TH

Diane took me to her apartment for lunch. She shares a one-bedroom place with her friend Robin, whom she knew in New York. They work together in that ironworks company. Their place is nicely decorated. Three pencil-drawn prints of little Rastafarian girls Diane brought back from Jamaica last year hung on the wall in the living room. They really stand out, those black girls in black frames against the long white wall. She also has a picture of John and me taken about thirty years ago. I must have been forty pounds heavier. I loved the suit I wore, and my hair. John looked almost the same in the picture as he did the day he died. My eyes are sunken now, but I remember them as they looked in the picture.

Diane told me that they pay four hundred and twenty-five dollars a month, including utilities. I can't imagine why; the place is small. Diane sleeps on the sofa bed and Robin has the bedroom.

When I got to their apartment Robin hugged me and kissed me on the cheek. How are you, Mother? she asked me. She has called me mother from the first day we met. Many of my children's friends call me mother. I like it.

Robin wore a pair of shorts that cut high up in her crotch and looked as if it would do damage when she walked. Creases and folds outlined areas I wouldn't want to call attention to. The children call me old-fashioned. Karen has called me inhibited. Only those who see know, and just because I don't like to show in public what I might in private doesn't mean I'm inhibited.

Robin and Diane are quite different, but they get along well and that's important. Diane put on a record, the Mighty Sparrow—that man can sing a calypso song. I could see Diane and Robin cooking from the open bar area dividing the living room from the kitchen. Diane looked out at me and asked if I was all right. I went to the counter to get a closer look at what we would be eating. Being with them was so pleasant. Besides, Mrs. Oliver deserved a break from taking care of two old women.

They put the food on the table, a good-looking meal. Robin made French onion soup and baked an apple pie. Diane cooked broiled chicken, rice and peas, broccoli and fried plantains. She mashed the broccoli and cut up the chicken in my plate. She had looked annoyed with Mrs. Oliver when she came to get me and saw I wasn't wearing my dentures. She calmed down when Mrs. Oliver told her I wouldn't keep them in and wouldn't open my mouth to let her put them in.

We sat at the table and said a short grace. We only said grace as a family on holidays, when Percy subjected us to his preaching and kept us standing while our food got cold. I ate a lot, and Diane and Robin were pleased. While they cleared the table I took a closer look at the pictures on the wall.

The day was going well until I slipped on an area rug, fell and bruised my forehead against the wall. Diane and Robin were beside themselves with worry. They carried me to the sofa and cleaned the cut with peroxide. I worried how the fall might affect my condition, but I didn't want to be a problem for the girls. They put me in the bedroom to rest before going back to Mrs. Oliver's.

Diane asked me if I enjoyed lunch when I woke up. It was the best I've had for a long time. I didn't mean the remark as a bad reflection on Mrs. Oliver because the woman is an excellent cook, but I liked being in Diane's place.

"Mother, we'll be going back to New York if I'm laid off," she said.

I didn't mind. Then Diane told me what was really bothering her.

Henry wasn't expecting me until January, and he and Lilly, his wife, have been taking care of her mother. When we move back to New York, I will have to stay with Thelma and Percy.

I don't want to stay with Thelma. I want to be with Henry and Lilly. I'm not comfortable around Thelma and Percy, both of them are steeped in their religion; they depress me with their talk about the afterlife. They don't consider how close I am to the grave. I don't want to be constantly reminded of it. I stayed with them before I came to Houston and had no intentions of going back. Their house is dark and solemn.

I asked Diane if I could stay with Karen and Angela. She said they were in Jamaica, and Sandra had rented out the bedroom in her basement. I was not comforted by Diane's assurances that I wouldn't have to stay with Thelma and Percy long. But she said Andrew begged her to come back, a good sign. I don't want her to miss her chance of being with Andrew.

"The Lord is my Shepherd." I don't know why the passage came into my head. I also remembered the name of that song that John sang—"Sentimental Journey." I started singing, and Diane laughed and sang with me. She remembered how much her father liked that song.

At six o'clock Diane took me back to Mrs. Oliver's. Mrs. Oliver put her arms around me and asked if I had a nice day. She apologized to Diane again about my dentures. Diane told her she should try to get me to wear them. Mrs. Oliver said she would, but I know she won't. Diane shouldn't worry. I'm eating; I'm not starving—I only look as if I am.

MONDAY, MARCH 12TH

Dorothy came to visit her aunt last evening. Miss Turner told her about the letter she had written to her friend Gertrude. Dorothy told her aunt that Gertrude died last year. Miss Turner's eyes narrowed. She said it was Brenda Williams who died last year. Brenda Williams and Gertrude Howard, Dorothy reminded her aunt.

It's been only a day since Miss Turner mailed her letter. Dorothy might have had the heart to let the letter be returned and not say anything.

After breakfast Miss Turner asked for more writing paper and a pen. She wrote a letter to a Jim Samuels. I wondered if she planned to share a place with him. John was the only man I have ever known, like that. I have done a lot of looking and wondering. I don't pay any mind to those ministers who say that we commit adultery in the mind as well as in the body. They carry things too far. A little diversion now and again, especially in the mind, doesn't do any harm. I think a lot of them are speaking from their own experience why they are so hot on the issue.

Clara brought Mrs. Price to visit on Tuesday. She hasn't been gone long but she has changed. Her hair hung close to her face in a greasy pageboy. She tiptoed into the living room and walked leaning to one side as if someone invisible were holding her up. Her face was puffy and her lips were chapped. She held out her hands to Mrs. Oliver, and I could see her fingers were swollen and her fingernails bitten way down. She sat down heavily on the sofa as if she had forgotten how low it was. She spread her legs far apart and I could see under her dress even though she sat with both hands on her knees. Mrs. Oliver asked her how she was. Mrs. Price wouldn't stop smiling. Her lips looked as if they would crack. The more I looked at her the stranger she became. Mrs. Oliver seemed to be changing her mind about keeping Mrs. Price. Clara might have dressed her mother in another color besides yellow. That smile, her sallow skin, her dress, she looked jaundiced. Before they left, I told Clara to put some Vaseline on her mother's lips. I thanked God for all my blessings after seeing Mrs. Price.

"Are you considering boarding that woman?" Miss Turner asked Mrs. Oliver.

"I used to keep Mrs. Price before you came here," Mrs. Oliver told her.

"That woman looks mad," Miss Turner said.

"What she needs is to get out of the hospital, get some good food and attention; she'll do just fine," Mrs. Oliver said.

"Your expectations are unrealistic. My niece brought me here because she says she is afraid of my getting hurt. And look at what I'm to live with."

Miss Turner was upset.

"She'll be in the back room. You won't have to worry, mam. I have taken care of worse. You're no bargain yourself," Mrs. Oliver said to Miss Turner.

Miss Turner is still waiting for her friend Gertrude to answer her letter. "What will I do if she is dead?" she cried. Mrs. Oliver told her crying wouldn't help. I told her she would hear from her friend Jim soon.

"He's probably dead too. That's all old people do, die, die, die."

"He might surprise you and be alive. Do you plan to stay with him?" I asked.

"Of course not. I want his sister's address; that's why I wrote."

"What if his sister is dead?" I don't know who told me to ask her that, pure deviltry. She moaned and Mrs. Oliver told her to keep quiet. I hope her Jim writes soon.

Miss Turner and I fell asleep in the living room. I woke up before she did. It felt good sitting near the door. A warm breeze blew through the screen. The shadow of the leaves spread over the top of the door, and looming in the leaves was a small figure that was growing larger. I leaned forward to get a better look and saw a young man standing at the door. I hadn't heard him come up the steps. That's how people get robbed in broad daylight.

"What do you want?" I asked. Miss Turner woke up then.

"Would you like to get *The Chronicle*, mam?" he asked, peering through the screen door.

"You'll have to ask Mrs. Oliver," I said.

"Yes, I would like to get the paper, on weekends too, thank you," Miss Turner said to the young man.

"Are you Mrs. Oliver?" the young man asked.

"Would I be ordering otherwise?"

She signed an order form. He told her delivery would start on Saturday; she would receive a statement once a month.

When he left, Miss Turner winked at me. Let her have her little victory. When Mrs. Oliver finds out, it will be another matter. I winked back at her.

Late in the afternoon Mrs. Oliver put us on the back porch, to get some fresh air. We were out for fifteen minutes when she came to take us in for an afternoon nap. I wasn't ready to go in. I could have used another hour of sun, but I have so little say these days. I don't want to complain, but I get sick of people controlling my life. Putting me out in the sun for fifteen minutes! I was sleeping fine at the dining room table before she took us out. Then she put me outside, and I began to get comfortable, watching the trees blow in the wind and looking at the pretty black birds, flying from fence to fence. One of the birds was slower than the other two, but it flew right along with them. They perched on the fence with their heads high. Just when I was beginning to fall asleep, she tells me it's time to come inside for a nap.

Miss Turner asked me what I write all the time. When I told her I was keeping a diary, she said she used to keep one years ago.

She asked what I could possibly find to write about since I was an old lady who did absolutely nothing but breathe, eat, sleep, belch and defecate.

I thought to tell her that was more than she was doing, but I think before I speak. I knew what I was thinking was better left unsaid.

WEDNESDAY, MARCH 14TH

My feet were swollen again this morning, but I didn't have any pain. Thelma called before lunch. Diane had called her last night, and Thelma wanted me to know she and Percy were ready for me. I told her I liked living in Houston and that Mrs. Oliver was a good person.

Diane called right after I talked with Thelma to tell me she would be over on Saturday. Everything was arranged with Thelma —no need for me to worry. I had figured I would be eighty before I went back to Thelma's. I had planned to ask Henry to keep me a little longer than he planned. I know he wouldn't have refused.

Thelma is a good person but since she got married and started going to church, she has become a fanatic. She and Percy have no regard for others' beliefs. Their religion is the "true religion." They don't allow pork to be eaten in their house, no iced tea and Bible study every night. I say my prayers before I go to sleep, just me and God. I like it that way. They think I enjoy it all. Because I am old, people expect me to be pious. I tried all my life to live decently and I thank God every day for giving me life, but Thelma has forgotten I'm not a pious person. They're likely to scare me to death.

Well, I'll take things as they come. Thelma is a soft soul; she wouldn't want to see her mother unhappy.

Diane hasn't told me when we are leaving for New York. Imagine my being moved from place to place at my age. I had left New York only once in thirty years. Since John died ten years ago, I have become a roadrunner. If I had gone before John, he wouldn't have put up with moving back and forth. He would have told the children to leave him in one place or put him in a home. The children would never have put him in a home.

Diane feels bad enough leaving me with Mrs. Oliver. I hate to threaten, but if things are too much at Thelma's, I might tell her to put me in a nursing home. It's terrible not having a choice about where I am to live; it is as if I was already dead.

I sat in the recliner almost all day with my legs raised. I could see my ankles and feet were swollen. Mrs. Oliver will probably call Diane. Such a waste of their time, diagnosing a little symptom here and there, mending this and that. I will never be as good as before.

My mind is filled with years of memories. I used to get annoyed with Auntie always talking about old times. I couldn't understand why she wanted to dwell on bad times, her men, what this one did and what the other one didn't. Then she would talk about that old broken-down house in the country her father left her. I asked her why she bothered to remember those things. Now I'm like her; I can't keep my mind on the present.

THURSDAY,
MARCH 15TH

I read my name in the front of my diary tonight.
Hortense *Nelson. When I say Hortense, it sounds strange, like someone I'm familiar with but don't really know. Hortense was part of the things I loved, taking care of the children and John, sewing, gardening, dancing, helping my friends. Mrs. Oliver calls me Mrs. Nelson, Mrs. Nelson, the old lady. Hortense, Hortense. I'm afraid I'll forget her along with everything else.*

Comfort me dear God. Maybe being with Thelma and Percy will be good. They're so sure of themselves. When they die, they will surely go to their heaven. And me?

Mrs. Oliver pulled back the covers and looked at my legs. They were not swollen, but they were stiff. She sat me up and leaned me against the bedboard with two pillows.

"So Mrs. Nelson is ready to go for a walk around the block. Your legs look fine," she said. She was talking to me like I wasn't there.

"You've never taken me for a walk in all the days I've been here. Today I feel like a corpse, and you want to walk. I'll take a walk tomorrow," I said.

"I'm only teasing. But if you feel well, we can take a short one tomorrow."

She massaged and brushed my scalp and braided my hair. After my bath she dressed me in one of my new dresses and new socks.

I heard her and Miss Turner arguing in the bathroom. They have these discussions every morning when it's Miss Turner's time to bathe. Miss Turner wants to be left alone in the bathroom. Mrs. Oliver refuses. She sits on the toilet seat and watches Miss Turner, telling her to wash under her arms, between her legs, so she won't smell. Miss Turner needs help getting out of the tub now. Two weeks ago she could do it herself. She is becoming an invalid before my eyes. Yesterday she spilled her coffee when she got her finger caught in the handle of the cup.

FRIDAY,
MARCH 16TH

Two ladies from Mrs. Oliver's church came to visit.
They gave Miss Turner and me each a bunch of pink and red
carnations. One of them, a fat woman with a big round face, read
the 121st Psalm, "I will lift up mine eyes unto the hills, from whence
cometh my help. My help cometh from the Lord, which made heaven
and earth..." She read with great feeling. I thought she would cry.
I felt as if I would too.

We had a late supper of spareribs and baked beans that
stayed on my chest all night. I had a terrible dream. I dreamt
Mrs. Oliver got me out of bed early, gave me a bath, put on my
blue suit and white blouse. She put a bib around my neck and
sat me at the table in front of a plate full of grits and four fried
eggs oozing yellow from their yolks.

Then she told me not to get anything on my clothes, that
I would want to look good for my trip. She wiped my mouth
when I was finished and took me to the bathroom. As we passed
my bedroom, I saw an old woman sitting on my bed. She smiled
at me with a toothless grin. I asked Mrs. Oliver who was sitting
on my bed; she told me it was her new patient.

I told her that my bed isn't even cold yet, and she already
had somebody else in it.

She didn't answer. I could have been speaking to myself.
Diane came in. I could hear her voice, but I could hardly see
her.

She called to me several times, "Mother, Mother."

I answered, but she didn't hear me.

She picked up the telephone. —Henry, I can't find Mother.

I rushed to her, walking strong and straight and took the
phone from her hand. —Henry, get rid of Lilly's mother. I'm

your mother, and I'm on my way to stay with you. Call Thelma and tell her not to expect me.

I didn't remember my dream when I first woke up. But it slowly came back to me. I would never think of calling Henry and saying such a thing; after all, Lilly's mother is an old helpless woman.

Mrs. Oliver smiled at me when she came in the bedroom.

"Diane is coming today, are you happy?"

I asked her if Diane had told her we were going back to New York. She knew all about it. I asked her if she had somebody else to take my bed.

"Not yet, but soon," she said.

"You won't let the bed get cold before you put another body in it."

She said she hoped the man or woman would be like me since I was no trouble.

"He? So you'll be running a coed foster home. Why did you wait until I'm leaving to do this?"

"They never had a man available before, you old fox," Mrs. Oliver laughed.

I thought about Miss Turner. If Mrs. Oliver had a male boarder who was not too far gone, he might be the answer to Miss Turner's problem.

Diane was pretty and happy. I told her how good she looked. She was relieved now that she could make plans. She was sorry we had to move again so soon. She said it was good getting away from New York, but everyone was glad we were coming back.

"Sometimes I forget where I am, Di. I think I'm sitting in my kitchen, then I look at all the junk Mrs. Oliver has and I remember." I don't know why I told her that.

Diane said the same thing happens to her when she wakes up and thinks she's in her bed in Queens, only the bed is in a different position, and she doesn't know which side to get off.

Diane told Mrs. Oliver we would be leaving on Wednesday morning, but she would be coming for me Monday evening. Before she left, she told me she and Robin would take me to dinner Tuesday night to the Ethiopian restaurant we never got to when she was sick.

The *Chronicle* was delivered today. Mrs. Oliver brought it in. She checked the sales section, refolded the paper, stuffed it back in the plastic bag and returned it to the porch.

SUNDAY,
MARCH 18TH

Mrs. Oliver shampooed and French braided my hair. She soaked my feet in Epsom salts to soften my hard thick toenails before she cut them. She trimmed and filed my fingernails and painted them with clear polish. I asked her if she had a polish with more color. She said she only had red which would be too bright for me. All this attention because I'm leaving.

The Chronicle *came again. Mrs. Oliver murmured to herself as she came into the living room with both Sunday and Saturday papers. She said she didn't know why they were suddenly leaving her papers and that she would call Monday morning. Miss Turner said if* The Chronicle *wanted to give her a free subscription, she shouldn't worry about it.*

Some people are honest, Mrs. Oliver told her.

She spread the Sunday paper on the floor. Miss Turner suggested Mrs. Oliver look over the employment section since I was leaving, and she would be gone soon. She said Mrs. Oliver would need something to do.

They're alike in some ways. Both of them are bullheaded, for one thing.

Mrs. Oliver saw me writing in my diary and said as soon as I was finished she was going to put it away in my suitcase. What's the rush; there was still tomorrow, I told her.

DEEANNE DAVIS is published in various anthologies as a poet, but this is her first published piece of fiction. In addition to working on this novel-in-progress, she is an editor and writes her own solo performance pieces. She has taught theatre workshops with youth, women and low-income adults. For the past eight years, she has worked as a marketing and media planner at the Public Media Center in San Francisco.

As a lesbian of american African descent, **GLORIA YAMATO** is settling into the satisfaction of writing for a living. She's worked for many years with social service and social change organizations. Her writing has appeared in anthologies and publications including *Diversity: The Lesbian Rag* and *Making Face Making Soul/Haciendo Caras.* Yamato recently completed a residency at Hedgebrook Cottages for Women Writers. She currently resides in the Bay Area.

RABIE HARRIS was born in Jamaica in 1944 and came to the U.S. in 1955. She has a BS in Sociology from Brooklyn College, a BA in English from Pace University and an MA in Creative Writing from the University of Houston. She is an adjunct instructor of English at the University of Houston, downtown, and also at Houston Community College.

SAUDA BURCH is a Black lesbian writer living in Oakland.

aunt lute books is a multicultural women's press that has been committed to publishing high quality, culturally diverse literature since 1982. In 1990, the Aunt Lute Foundation was formed as a non-profit corporation to publish and distribute books that reflect the complex truths of women's lives and the possibilities for personal and social change. We seek work that explores the specificities of the very different histories from which we come, and that examines the intersections between the borders we all inhabit.

Please write or phone for a free catalogue of our other books or if you wish to be on our mailing list for future titles. You may buy books directly from us by phoning in a credit card order or mailing a check with the catalogue order form.

Aunt Lute Books
P. O. Box 410687
San Francisco, CA 94141
(415) 826-1300

This Book would not have been possible without the kind contributions of the *Aunt Lute Founding Friends:*

Anonymous Donor   Diana Harris
Anonymous Donor   Phoebe Robins Hunter
Rusty Barcelo   Diane Mosbacher, M.D., Ph.D.
Marian Bremer   William Preston, Jr.
Diane Goldstein   Elise Rymer Turner